*Other Series by Harper Lin*

The Patisserie Mysteries

The Emma Wild Holiday Mysteries

The Wonder Cats Mysteries

The Emma Wild Mysteries

**www.HarperLin.com**

# A Deadly Bridal Shower

A Pink Cupcake Mystery Book 2

Harper Lin

ISBN-13: 978-1987859362
ISBN-10: 1987859367

# Contents

# Chapter One

"I don't know why I'm so nervous." Amelia sighed into her Bluetooth as she drove the Pink Cupcake truck down Meridian Street. Her appointment was taking her toward a house in a neighborhood she had never been to. "You should see the homes around here, Lila. They look like mansions. I don't even want to think about the property taxes these people pay."

Amelia smoothed the hair on the top of her head and felt the band that was holding it all back in a tight ponytail. She wondered if she should have worn something a little more professional instead of jeans and a hot-pink T-shirt that matched her truck. It was as close to a uniform as she had. Money was good, but she wasn't at the point of company tees yet.

A year and a half ago, the Pink Cupcake food truck had been just a vague idea. What did a newly divorced woman in her mid-forties with two teenagers know about running a food-truck business?

Yet, here she was. Despite the discouragement from her ex-husband, despite the hoops the city made her jump through, and despite her harshest, most merciless critic—herself—she was sole owner of the Pink Cupcake.

The truck had been stationed in its same little spot on Food Truck Alley for over six months. Its hot-pink signature paint would have caught anyone's eye immediately, but slowly, it was the cupcakes that were becoming the main attraction.

They were delicious combinations of unique flavors like ginger-and-orange glazed lemon cupcakes or traditional chocolate cupcakes, the size of softballs, that people were soon lining up for every day during the morning rush and lunch hour.

Business had become so good that some days, Amelia had to send Lila home early and pull the truck out because they had baked every bit of flour, spread every last scoop of icing, and used every edible decoration they had on stock for that day.

However, even with all of her success so far, this drive had her stomach in nervous knots.

"Lila, these houses could eat my house as a small appetizer."

This stretch of Gary, Oregon, was known as Sarkis Estates. It made Amelia's previous home with her ex-husband, John, look like a slum. But Amelia would never say that out loud and risk coming across like a snob to her employee, Lila. Actually, Lila was much more than just an employee. Right now she was playing the role of personal cheerleader.

"So what? Big houses? Big deal."

"I think I just saw a Bentley! A Bentley, Lila! Are you kidding me?"

"Sorry, but none of those cars match the hot set of wheels you're driving."

Amelia laughed out loud.

The Pink Cupcake stood out like a sideshow attraction at a funeral. Small children who had been busy playing in their front yards or walking along the sidewalks would stop and wave as if they had caught part of a parade going by. Older people would look with surprise or even distaste as the hot-pink machine rolled past, but Amelia was too jittery to care.

"Gosh, for such a ritzy area, you'd think the streets would be smoother. I've got to drive fifteen miles an hour so as not to jostle my precious cargo."

"Just take your time. Anyone in a hurry can pass you," Lila encouraged. "You know I would have gone with you except that I made this appointment with the doctor months ago."

"I wish you would have told me sooner. I would have scheduled things differently and gone with you."

"It's for a checkup. Nothing more," Lila said, sounding annoyed. "I've been going to the doctor's office alone for over twenty years. If I all of a sudden start showing up with an entourage, I may break my winning streak."

"Winning streak? It's what friends do. Besides, that way I could have brought you with me to this tasting. You made this happen, not me. Whose shoulder will I cry on if they spit out my cupcakes?"

Over the past couple of weeks, Amelia had come to consider Lila like family. She was a reliable employee whose way with numbers was proving to be invaluable. Every cent was accounted for, as Lila had promised in her interview, but she also was helping Amelia with small ways to invest back in the business to ensure a greater savings. Plus, she had a good heart.

The Pink Cupcake lumbered from side to side, bouncing groggily over each manhole cover or stuffed pothole.

"These cupcakes are never going to make it." Amelia squeezed the steering wheel until her knuckles were white. "They are going to be stuck to the tops of the boxes."

"No, I put tall toothpicks in each box to prevent just that from happening."

Amelia shook her head and smiled. "You thought of everything. You're like my guardian angel. I owe you so much."

Today was the day her catering career either took off or crashed. She was headed to the home of Mr. and Mrs. Miller, the parents of Darcy Miller, the bride-to-be who was looking for something unusual but delicious for her bridal party.

"They are just regular people," Lila soothed from the other end of the line.

"Yeah, regular people with Bentleys, Jaguars, and Mercedes in their driveways. You know, I bet each house has at least four bathrooms."

"Amelia, none of that matters. You have the one thing they want." Lila continued her pep talk. "That is, the world's best cupcakes. They don't have that. All their money and they have never tasted anything like your chocolate raspberry truffle cupcake or the sinfully delicious vanilla and strawberry glaze cupcake or the surprisingly simple yet elegant PB and J cupcake, my personal favorite."

Amelia laughed out loud since Lila was the one who had thought up the peanut-butter-and-jelly cupcake.

"Surprisingly simple yet elegant? Like its creator?"

Now it was Lila's turn to laugh.

Her eyes passed over the beautifully manicured lawns and tended flower beds.

Huge trees indicated most of the homes had been there for a long time. Slowing the truck down a little more so as not to jostle the cupcakes, Amelia quickly glanced at the directions she had printed out and looked up at the next road sign.

"Okay, I think I'm...What the heck?" A low rumble like thunder could be heard over the truck engine. Amelia listened. Her first thought was to look up. In all the old science fiction movies she'd watched with her kids, alien abductions always started with a weird hum that got louder and louder. Just like this.

"What is that noise?" Lila asked.

"I can't believe you can hear that. I think... it's someone's stereo."

The deep bass of oversized woofers was quickly approaching the truck. Amelia could not only hear the annoying sound but also felt the thumping through her steering wheel.

Looking in the rearview mirror, Amelia saw a car quickly approaching.

"Oh my gosh. I'll give you one guess as to what darling little girl is making all that noise," Amelia hollered, her voice nearly drowned out by the awful music.

"It sounds like the mother ship is landing!" Lila shouted.

"What is wrong with this person?"

"Is that that girl with the red Corvette?"

"And you win the million-dollar question! Yup! Dana Foster!" Amelia shouted as the car quickly sped up to her truck, honking the horn and revving the engine.

"You'd think she would have learned her lesson after having her name all over the police blotter a couple of months ago," Lila yelled over the noise.

"Are you kidding? Any attention is good attention to a girl like her."

"That's a girl whose parents should have taken a wooden spoon to her behind years ago."

"You mean Kane and Millicent Foster? Those two are never around. Always jet-setting to the farthest ends of the globe, at least that's what I've heard."

Pursing her lips and shaking her head slightly, Amelia watched Dana Foster inch closer and closer to the back of her truck, then fall back only to charge up to her bumper again.

"She's going to cause an accident!" Amelia shouted into the phone. "I gotta go."

"Call me when it's over," Lila shouted back then disconnected the line.

Amelia tried to concentrate on where she was going, but the pounding bass, the gunning engine, and the blonde yelling heaven knew what obscenities at Amelia was such a distraction that she was afraid the red Corvette was going to plow right into her. There was another girl that Amelia didn't recognize in the car, who was laughing hysterically.

Both girls were wearing large sunglasses that made them look like exotic bugs. Their hair whipped wildly out of the open convertible top, and the passenger, pretending it was a roller-coaster ride, had both of her arms up over her head, hooting and hollering.

Finally, the solid double line in the middle of the road became a series of dashes, and the Corvette immediately swerved around the Pink Cupcake.

"Learn how to drive, lady!" Dana shouted as she stayed parallel with the truck. "You.... get off the....road!"

She continued to harass Amelia, who, being more than familiar with the girl's antics, kept her face looking pleasant and barely glanced in her direction. But while looking straight ahead and watching the road, Amelia saw what neither Dana nor her friend did. And there was an oncoming car.

"Stupid...nice truck...crazy...!"

Normally Amelia wouldn't pay any attention to foul-mouthed, wet-behind-the-ears "new" adults, but it was obvious that the girls weren't paying attention. Amelia pointed out her front windshield and looked toward the Corvette.

She slowed the truck so the sports car could pass, but Dana slowed down, too, just to continue her abusive tirade.

"Look out!" Amelia shouted.

Still Dana stared at the pink truck, jerking the steering wheel every time, making the engine roar as she hit the accelerator every few seconds.

"There's a car coming!" Amelia pointed, her eyes wide.

The other driver honked but didn't slow down.

"Where'd you learn how to drive, lady?"

Amelia stared in disbelief at Dana, back up at the other car, back at Dana, and finally at the road in front of her.

It didn't even occur to Dana why her friend was pounding on her arm, trying to get her attention. She wasn't laughing anymore. She was nearly crying.

Finally paying attention to the road, Dana heard the horn of the oncoming car, only to push the gas all the way to the floor, zoom past Amelia—waving her middle finger in the process—and cutting in front of her just in time to miss the other car, which swerved off the road, kicking up dust and dirt, nearly losing control.

"That girl is going to get herself killed someday," Amelia grumbled to herself.

# Chapter Two

"How did it go, Mom?" Meg came bounding out of the house as Amelia pulled into the driveway. Amelia's daughter flipped her long, chestnut-colored hair behind her and helped her mom out of the truck.

"Well, it looks like the Pink Cupcake has its first catering job," Amelia said, smiling down at her daughter.

"That's great!" Wrapping her arms around her mother, Meg inched up on her tiptoes and kissed her on the cheek. "I knew you'd get it."

"I wish I had your confidence. Now all I have to do is bake one hundred peanut-butter-and-jelly cupcakes for Darcy

Miller's bridal party, which is being held at the Twisted Spoke in a week."

Wrinkling up her nose, Meg jerked her head back as if a fly had flown too close to her face.

"The Twisted Spoke? The place that used to be a garage? There are always a bunch of motorcycles parked outside."

Amelia rolled her eyes. The Twisted Spoke had been a garage at one time but now was a restaurant with garage doors that rolled all the way up, making most of the restaurant alfresco. The entire décor was leather and chrome, with the Harley-Davidson logo plastered on almost every square inch of the place. Food was served on paper plates, but the beer was poured into mason jars. The clientele varied during the day from business people on their lunch hour to families enjoying a dinner of burgers, but as the sun went down each night, a different kind of people started to take up space at the bar. The kind of people with prison tattoos, cigarette breath, bloodshot eyes—and that was just the females.

"The bride wanted something different."

"Yikes."

"She and her fiancé both have motorcycles. It's their *thing.*" Amelia shrugged. "She told me they were going to Sturgis for their honeymoon."

"What's Sturgis?"

"Sturgis is in South Dakota. Every year they have a big motorcycle rally, and thousands and thousands of bikers show up to, I don't know, have a party." Saying people went to Sturgis to "have a party" was like saying the Grand Canyon was an interesting plot of land, but Amelia didn't think her fourteen-year-old daughter needed to know the gory details of this yearly biker event.

"I've seen bikers before." Meg nodded her head.

"You have? Where?"

"*The Wild One* with Marlon Brando. Isn't that what bikers are like?"

Amelia nearly burst out laughing but instead just smiled at her daughter. *Let her think bikers really look like Marlon Brando. She'll run screaming in the opposite direction when she catches sight of a real one.*

"There might be one or two like that."

"Can I help you work the truck, Mom? I promise to be good and do whatever you ask. You won't even have to pay me."

Amelia twisted her daughter's long hair around her hand as they walked into the house.

"I'd love to have you, Meg, but this is the first catering job. Let me get my feet wet. The next one, I promise. I'll even pay you."

Meg slouched for a moment but after hearing the words "I'll even pay you," snapped her head up and smiled.

"Okay."

"Where's your brother?"

"In the dungeon, where else?" Meg chirped, bounding up the stairs to her bedroom.

Making her way to the kitchen, Amelia rubbed her head. Her temples had been throbbing since that red Corvette sped past her. Actually, Amelia couldn't blame the reckless Dana Foster for her headache. It was stress induced.

The preparation for the meeting with the Millers, the baking of sixteen perfect cupcakes, the harrowing drive to their house, the intimidation of their neighborhood, the party details and the price—Lord, the price that she'd waffled back and forth on. It all had taken its toll, but now the hard part was over. She had gotten the job. She had gotten the job for a fantastic price that would ease the burden of bills for the next two months.

"Adam!" she called toward the closed basement door.

Within a few minutes, she heard the pounding of her son's feet going up the stairs. The door swung open, and there he was.

"What's up, Mom?" He brushed his wavy black hair to the side. "Did you get the catering job?"

"I sure did." Amelia's voice was quiet.

"That's awesome!"

"Yeah, thanks." She reached out and mussed his hair. "Would you mind posting a Tweet for me? I'd like to get it out there. Mention it's the original peanut-butter-and-jelly cupcake and the first catering job and anything else that might sound nice."

"Sure. I'll add some pictures, too."

"Thank you, honey. I've got a headache a mile long. I was so nervous, my system is just relieved to have it all over."

"When cupcakes taste as good as yours do, Mom, it should have been the customer who was nervous you wouldn't cater their party." Adam turned and headed back down into the basement where he practically lived all the hours he wasn't either in school or outside skateboarding.

Adam's comment brought tears to Amelia's eyes, but she didn't cry. Despite her headache, she felt too good to cry. How many nights after her divorce had she lain awake at night wondering how she was going to make ends meet if her cupcake business didn't work out? How many times had she imagined filing bankruptcy or standing in line for welfare? She had imagined a thousand different failures and made plans to survive every one of them. Never in her wildest dreams had she planned for how to handle success. It wasn't that Amelia had never experienced success before. It was just that this was real success that she had accomplished without her ex-husband's help.

John had made it clear he wasn't happy about her business. An ex-wife who drove a food truck was not as respectable, she supposed, as the waitressing career his mistress, Jennifer, had. However, Jennifer's restaurant or bar or whatever it was didn't make it on the news because a dead body hadn't been found near it, as had happened with the Pink Cupcake, but that was another story altogether.

The thought made her click her tongue and chuckle as she went upstairs to her room. Peeling off her clothes and slipping into some comfy pajamas, Amelia looked at her reflection in the dresser mirror. Suddenly a thought so devious, so indulgent, and so wild entered into her head that it made her gasp.

"I'm going to cut my hair."

# Chapter Three

"I think it looks amazing!" Lila gushed, smoothing the short pixie cut Amelia had gotten the night before.

"You don't think it's too short? I don't look like a boy?" Amelia fretted as she patted the back of her neck.

"With your figure?" Lila rolled her eyes. "Even a blind man would know you were all woman."

Smiling, Amelia nudged Lila with her elbow as they prepared the cupcakes outside the Twisted Spoke. It was a beautiful gray day, typical for Gary, Oregon.

The hot-pink truck looked like an exotic blossom positioned in the parking lot next to the rustic building. With their window open, Amelia and Lila faced the restaurant so the bridal shower guests could easily walk up to help themselves to the biker-themed delectables.

Despite the fact that Amelia would never want a biker-themed anything, the open area of the Twisted Spoke looked great. There were two picnic tables for the bride, the mothers, and the bridesmaids. The rest of the guests were at tables for four with stickers and paper fans and trinkets scattered across the tops, to be used for what would obviously be bridal shower games. There was nothing too frilly, but there were small, elegant flower arrangements of black and silver in the middle of each table. Amelia thought the decorations and restaurant looked oddly complementary.

As the ovens were starting to give off the sweet aroma of yellow cake with vanilla and peanut butter, a high-strung Mrs. Tabitha Miller, mother of the bride, came bustling up to the window. Her beautifully French-manicured nails clicked on the counter.

"Hello!" she squealed. "Everything going all right?"

Amelia came to the open window and leaned out to talk.

"Hello, Tabitha. Everything is just fine. How are you holding up?" She could smell a bit of alcohol on the woman already and was sure the party had started before they arrived at the biker restaurant.

"Well, one little snag," she said, frowning like she was posing for one of those awful clown paintings. "It seems that my husband's cousin and her three grown daughters are coming after all. Our neighbors have also had a change in plans and decided they will more than likely stop by. Do you think we'll have enough to accommodate them?" She swayed just a little as she waited for Amelia to reply, her eyes slightly bloodshot.

"I'll make the adjustment, Tabitha. We're prepared to handle things like this," Amelia said sweetly while clenching her fists at her sides.

"That's great! Can I get you a Bloody Mary? They are absolutely delicious."

"No, thank you," Amelia replied, feeling the contagious giggles spreading from Lila, who was out of view behind her by the open back door.

"Okay then!" She clapped her hands together. "Can't wait to see everyone's faces when they taste your cupcakes! Peanut butter and jelly! Yum!"

As Tabitha wobbled away, Amelia turned and looked at Lila, who was silently laughing until the woman was out of hearing range and safely planted back at the bar.

"This is the third time she has changed the number of guests coming. I've kept meticulous records of everything. People who have money are very reluctant to pay for changes and inconveniences they caused." Amelia shook her head. "Thank goodness I have you as a witness."

"This is going to be the best party ever! I should have brought my camera." Lila bounced on her toes.

"Please don't tell me you are in the blackmail business, because that is the only reason I could think of for taking any pictures of this."

"Not anymore," Lila quipped without skipping a beat. "But you should have some pictures for your website and stuff."

Amelia thought a moment and then nodded her head.

"That's a really good idea. John is picking up the kids today. He can swing by on his way home and let Adam take a few snaps, then be on his way." Pulling her phone out of her pocket, she dialed her ex-husband's number, but as soon as he answered, Amelia felt the need to inch her way closer to the front of the truck and away from Lila, the window, and everyone.

"John, it's on the way. I'm not asking you to stay. I'm not even asking you to turn the engine off. I'm asking for a quick favor that will only take five minutes."

"Well, Amelia, it's a real inconvenience, but if you're going to make an issue..."

"I'm going to pretend you didn't say that. The guests will already be here when you arrive. Just pull up in front and you'll see the truck. Adam can..."

"Yeah, you can't miss that truck."

Amelia bit her tongue. This was a good day for her, a special day. Why John couldn't be happy for her, she didn't know and didn't have time to worry about. "Thanks, John," she snapped. "Adam will know what to do." With that she hit the End Call button and took a deep breath.

"Everything okay?" Lila asked.

"Yes." Amelia spat out the word as if it tasted bad in her mouth.

"It's going to take him a while to get used to it," Lila said while pulling down the tubes of silver candies and sprinkles Amelia had bought for the Miller bridal shower cupcakes.

"Get used to what?"

"You getting along without him. Maybe even flourishing." Lila waved her hands in a swooping motion over her head.

"He doesn't love me anymore. Hasn't for a while. I'm okay with that. Isn't that what he wants?" Amelia peeked in the oven windows and checked her watch.

"I think you might be confusing what he wants with what you want." Lila laughed as she spoke. "Has he seen your hair?"

Amelia squared her shoulders, and a sly smirk crept over her lips.

"Nope." She grinned openly. "He hasn't ever seen me with hair above my shoulders."

"Well, he's in for a shock." Lila popped one of the silver candies in her mouth before both of them began to work on the frosting and designs.

Slowly the guests started to arrive, and Amelia was surprised that she knew a couple of them. There was Mrs. Glenda Toedale—whom Amelia's kids called Toenail—who worked at the library. Sadie Lucas was on the Gary Community Council that John had been a member of. Sadie had elaborate Christmas parties and had offered Amelia some very kind words after the divorce was made public.

"You're better off" was all she said, with a hug and a knowing look. Someday, Amelia thought she might ask her about that, but today was not that day.

The most interesting guest was Mrs. O'Toole. She was an eccentric old woman who was rumored to have buried gold bars in the walls of her house. She was wearing her raincoat as a dress. She had been married to the same man for over forty years, but he was rarely seen anymore. The plight of the elderly.

Deep in conversation and up to their elbows in decorating, both Amelia and Lila jumped when a gruff voice coughed and sputtered at the back door of the truck.

"Excuse me, Amelia."

Amelia looked up and saw the manager of the Twisted Spoke smiling at them. It was obvious that a lifetime of riding on the open road had permanently weathered his face. His wild red hair was pulled back in a ponytail, and his beard was trimmed close to his wide jowl. His T-shirt had an American flag, a bike, and some message about freedom. He smelled like a country barbeque. No resemblance to Marlon Brando at all.

"Hey, Rusty." Amelia waved and quickly scooted around Lila to go shake his hand. "Thanks for the accommodations here. This is a perfect spot."

"Well, I'm happy to work with you. I just wanted to let you ladies know that lunch is on me. I'll have a couple of burgers delivered around as soon as my guy is done preparing them. I thought it might be better if you eat now. I saw the mother in there." Rusty jerked his head toward Tabitha. "This is going to be one of those real barn burners."

Amelia laughed and nodded her head in agreement.

"Rusty, this is my friend Lila Bergman." She stepped back to allow Lila to shake Rusty's hand. From the look on his face, it was obvious he hadn't expected the view to be so nice. Amelia couldn't picture Lila on the back of a Harley, but a year ago, she wouldn't have pictured herself running her own business, so what did she know?

"Can I get you ladies anything to drink? Coke? Beer? Tequila?" He looked at Lila, who smiled and planted her hands on her hips, shaking her head no.

"I think we're good, Rusty. Thank you."

"Well, I'll be back around to check on you. Let me know if you need anything." He gave a quick salute as he stepped off the back step but not before his eyes took inventory of Lila's backside.

"Oh, now, that is smitten!" Amelia shook her head and clicked her tongue as if it were such a shame. "He's going to invite you for a ride on his Harley. You know he is." Thoughts about John, his attitude, and his arrival were already forgotten.

"You say that as if I've never been on one," Lila said, barely looking up from her decorating task.

Gasping and covering her mouth, Amelia started to laugh. Then Lila did, too. It was like two high school girls gossiping about a senior football player at the pep rally.

Before they knew it, all the guests were seated in plain view of the truck. Some of the women pointed, some laughed, and some gasped, but half a dozen of them said they had seen the Pink Cupcake parked at Food Truck Alley, and a few more had said they had eaten from there.

Words like *delicious*, *amazing* and *sooo good* were used when describing their experiences, but Amelia pretended she didn't hear. She stayed focused and soon had a beautiful arrangement of over seventy-five giant peanut-butter-and-jelly cupcakes with a hint of vanilla, white cream cheese frosting, silver confetti sprinkles, black and silver edible flowers, and tiny silver beads that sparkled like gems in the center. Everything perched daintily in the hot-pink boats the cupcakes could be carried in.

Rusty brought Amelia and Lila two of the biggest burgers they had ever seen with french fries, onion rings, and dill pickles.

Unaware of how hungry they were, they devoured the meals just as the guests of the bridal shower were beginning to play their first game. They broke up into groups, and each was given several rolls of toilet paper to construct a wedding dress. They'd be scored on originality, neatness, and overall appearance. The wild laughter was contagious.

"Sounds like they're having a blast." Amelia laughed as she wiped her hands on her apron.

But as quickly as the laughter escalated, it died down only to be replaced by a familiar sound that made Amelia stop and hold her breath.

# Chapter Four

"Yikes!" Lila folded her arms over her chest. "I don't believe it."

"I know that sound. Where have I...?" Leaning out of the back door of the truck, Amelia saw a familiar sight. A red Corvette pumping out the worst, most chest-pounding, headache-inducing music was parking right in front of the Pink Cupcake.

"Dana Foster." Now it was Lila who was shaking her head. She wasn't the only one.

The gaggle of women had almost completely stopped what they were doing as they watched the blonde pour herself out of her car and saunter toward the restaurant, wearing short shorts and a white T-shirt so tight there was nothing left to the imagination.

Oblivious to everyone, and apparently having let it slip her mind that she had harassed a woman who drove a truck identical to the one parked next to the Twisted Spoke, Dana strolled past, into the bar area, and disappeared behind the Employees Only sign.

"She works here?" Lila squawked. "Good thing we already ate. I wouldn't trust that piece of work around my food."

Judging by the reaction of the crowd, there were some ladies who weren't exactly thrilled to see the twenty-something, either.

"I wonder what the hubbub is all about?" Amelia scratched her chin.

"I'll go find out." Lila slipped down the steps and strolled into the party to seek out Darcy. It was her conversation with the officer manning the Gary Police Department front desk that had gotten this whole catering ball rolling.

Darcy stood up and hugged Lila. They talked, and it was obvious that Darcy was introducing her to the ladies, waving her hands and pointing and showing off her ring again. They both turned toward the truck, and Amelia gave a friendly wave and smiled.

Looking around as Lila and Darcy spoke, Amelia noticed movement out of the corner of her eye. Leaning slightly toward the window, she saw three of the guests standing away from the main party. One of the girls was crying while the other two tried to talk to her.

"Don't pay any attention to her. She's just trying to upset you," the shortest girl in the group said while patting the crier on the back.

"Yeah. Besides, she wants you to say something to her. She thrives on drama. That's all she has." The third girl was lighting a cigarette and blew the smoke high up over her friends' heads.

"Give me one of those," the crier said. "I just can't believe she's here. How can she even show her face?"

"She probably didn't know you were going to be here," Shorty soothed.

"She'd have to know. The party was under Miller Bridal Shower. How many Millers are in this town getting married?

Everyone knows we are friends with Darcy," the smoker added while lighting the crier's cigarette.

"Look, everyone knows she's a slut and a liar. And it isn't just us. She's been around with so many guys that..." Shorty started but was, well, cut short.

"But I don't care about other guys. I cared about Cole." The crier took a deep drag and cried out the smoke in spasms. "She ruined it. I hate her! I wish she was dead!"

The smoker dropped her cigarette and embraced the crier, who sobbed almost hysterically on her shoulder. Shorty ran inside and grabbed a beer. Tapping the crier on the shoulder, she handed her the bottle and watched as her friend tilted her head back and chugged the entire brewski.

"That ought to help," Amelia muttered, pretending to be busy while continuing to listen.

"Look, girls like Dana Foster always get what's coming to them. Maybe not today but eventually," Shorty stated with her hands on her hips.

"That's right," the smoker concurred.

"I hate her so much." The crier wiped her eyes, careful to keep as much mascara and liner as possible unsmudged. "If I thought I could get away with it, I'd kill her myself."

"And we'd be right there to help you," Shorty added.

"That's right," the smoker concurred again.

Amelia shook her head sadly. She would have liked to tell the crier that it hurt for a little while, maybe a long while, but you got over it. Life got better. Men were like buses. If you missed one, another one came along sooner or later. Plenty of fish in the sea. "One man's trash is another man's treasure" or whatever other words of wisdom could be used to soothe a wounded heart.

"Hey, Mom." Adam's voice broke her train of thought. She whirled around and saw her son in the back door, holding his camera.

"Hi. Boy, thanks for coming by. I didn't even think about taking pictures for the website until Lila mentioned it." She gave him a quick squeeze. "You better just snap a few quick ones. We don't want to keep your father waiting."

"I don't think Dad would mind. It's Jennifer who's got ants in her pants." Adam rolled his eyes.

*More than that*, Amelia mused, but she didn't utter a word.

"Well, either way. Here." She pulled the tray of cupcakes in front of him. "What do you think?" It irked her that that woman-slash-girl was in the car with her children, but she was not going to make a scene. There was already enough female drama going on. Adding to it would be scandalous.

"These are so cool! Can I have this for my party?"

"Sure. Party? What party?"

"Dad said I could have a party when I turned seventeen," he said, snapping away a few pictures. "Should I get the crowd, too? If I include the logo of the restaurant, maybe the owner will put you on his website? Easy enough to ask."

"What kind of party?"

"At the Windham, downtown," Adam said innocently.

"Take a few snaps of whatever you think is best. As for this party, we'll talk. Seventeen-year-olds don't get parties at hotels. I don't even get to have a party at a hotel, and I deserve one."

"Mom," Adam groaned. "It's no big deal."

"I'm not signing off on anything. We'll talk. Your birthday is still a few months away."

"It won't cost you anything. Dad said…"

"Dad didn't say a word to me," Amelia replied firmly. "What did I say? Just because we don't live together doesn't mean we don't work together when it comes to you kids. Now I don't want to throw the hammer down, but I will if you keep pushing."

"Okay." Adam sighed. "I'll get a few pictures inside and around, and then I better go."

Amelia nodded, folding her arms over her chest and pursing her lips together. Following her son out, she looked toward the street and saw John's Suburban with its hazard lights blinking.

Jennifer was looking down, but Amelia could see a clear image of her ex-husband, who was anxiously sitting in the driver's seat. She pointed at him then made her hand into a phone, mouthing the words "call me." The look on her face must have conveyed her current mood because all John did was nod his head. Or maybe it was shock over her haircut. Either way, she had words for John, and he knew it.

Watching Adam get off a few pictures on his digital camera made Amelia wonder where all the time had gone. Wasn't he just a baby yesterday? He turned around and gave her that pitiful look all teenagers had perfected.

"I better go," he mumbled, forcing only the tiniest grin.

"Thank you for helping me," Amelia said, standing in his way. "We'll talk about your party, and I'm sure we'll come up with something."

Reluctantly, he smiled and nodded his head.

"Everything looks great, Mom!" he called out over his shoulder as he jogged back to where his father was parked.

"Hi, Mom!" yelled Meg from inside the car.

Amelia smiled, waved, and blew kisses as the car pulled away.

# Chapter Five

Amelia walked over to where Darcy and Lila were standing. After a few routine compliments about the decorations and everyone's appearance, Amelia asked when they'd like the cupcakes served.

"Oh, you know, we've got the place for about three hours. We're enjoying our premeal cocktails now. Then we'll all have lunch, with more cocktails." Darcy giggled and gave Amelia a gentle nudge with her elbow. "There are a few more games to play. I think whenever they want them, maybe they could help themselves. Just walk up to the truck? Or could you put them on the table over here? That would be perfect. Right, Mom?"

Tabitha whirled around, even more wobbly than before, batted her eyelashes, and smiled broadly.

"Anything you like, dear. My daughter, the police officer. She's going to be married. She's not a baby anymore." Tabitha's eyes welled.

"Mom, I've been carrying a gun to work for the past four years." Darcy looked at Amelia and Lila, rolling her eyes high up into her head. "I'm going to end up bringing her to the station and throwing her in the drunk tank, I just know it."

"You just take care of your mom, and we'll get the sweets." Amelia laughed.

Wishing the ladies a fun afternoon, she and Lila went back to the truck, grabbed the finished cupcakes, placed them in their displays on the table Darcy had indicated for the women to see, and listened to all the gushing exclamations.

"Oh, wow!"

"Those are so lovely!"

"Can you eat the flowers?"

"That will taste so good with my Manhattan!"

Without drawing any extra attention to herself, Amelia slipped a small stack of business cards next to the pretty pink trays and walked back to the truck with Lila, but before she got two steps away from the partygoers, the sound of shouts and swearing came from the left.

For a minute, Amelia thought someone was shouting at her. Who that she knew used that kind of language? No one. When she turned, she saw the offensive tirade was coming from Dana Foster, who was cornered near the back of the bar and as angry as a bear that had just been poked with a stick.

"If you're going to call me names, have the guts to say it to my face!" she shouted at the girl Amelia had seen crying with her two friends. It was pretty obvious from the way The Crier swayed that she had downed a few more drinks after she guzzled that beer.

"What are you going to do about it?" The Crier spat, holding her arms out wide at her sides, one hand holding a pink drink that looked like a cosmopolitan. "It isn't like you know how to do anything other than lie on your back. You're not even a good waitress."

The Crier's words were a little slurred, but everyone knew loud and clear what the meaning was. Dana didn't seem fazed at all. Amelia stood stone still, not sure if she should get involved, leave it to the bridal party or the owner, or just go back to the truck.

"Well, someone has to take care of Cole Hansen. Tell me again when you guys are supposed to get married? Oh, yeah. That's right. He dumped you for me. Then I dumped him. I remember." Dana nodded her head, her pretty blond hair bobbing up and down with it.

Without warning, The Crier threw her cosmopolitan in Dana's face. From where Amelia was standing, she could see it was obvious the second the liquid left the glass that The Crier regretted her action, but there was no use crying over spilled cosmos. She turned to make a quick getaway, but Dana was faster and more sober.

With catlike reflexes, Dana grabbed a handful of The Crier's hair, and the fight began. There were a few screams, half a dozen curse words, and finally the booming voices of police officer Darcy, the mother of the bride, and Rusty, who pulled Dana back by slipping his arm around her waist and yanking her away from her completely mismatched opponent. Shorty and The Smoker got in front of The Crier, who was really crying now, with her hair messed up and black streaks of mascara covering her cheeks. The guests were all on their feet, looking to see what had happened.

Mrs. O'Toole was the only one who didn't seem to care as she strolled casually up to the table of cupcakes, took one, and began to devour it as if she hadn't eaten in a week. It must have been good because she took another one and headed back to her seat, her raincoat reflecting the red-and-blue Pabst Blue Ribbon light closest to the bar.

"You get in the kitchen!" Rusty yelled at Dana.

"She started it!" Dana pointed at The Crier. "She threw a drink at me after calling me a..."

"I said get in the kitchen!" he barked, rubbing his face.

Dana gave him a steamy glare and stomped off through the Employees Only door.

"She should be fired!" The Crier yelled in between gulps of air.

"What in the world happened out here?" Rusty said, looking at everyone standing around.

"She jumped at me!"

Amelia shook her head, but before she could say anything, Lila stepped up from behind her.

"I'm sorry, but I think a little more than that took place." She didn't look at Amelia for permission but stepped right up to Rusty. "There was some kind of history between those two. Words were exchanged, yes, but I'm afraid this young lady threw her drink on your employee first."

"It's true. I saw it," Darcy concurred, nodding her head at Lila. "What in the world is the matter with you?" She looked at The Crier and shrugged her shoulders.

The Crier just cried some more and let Shorty and The Smoker lead her to an unoccupied picnic table where she sat down.

"Some black coffee might be in order." Lila grinned at Rusty, touching him lightly on the arm. He gave her a serious wink before going behind the bar to put on a fresh pot.

Darcy turned to her guests, smiling. There were other brides-to-be who would have been mortified over an altercation like this. They had made television shows about spoiled little girls who would freak out over a lesser offense like a broken nail or a droopy bouquet.

"All right." She shouted, "Let's everybody remember what is important here...me... okay?" Her guests laughed. "I think it's time we eat and open presents. Nothing makes people feel better quite like watching *me* open presents."

Even Amelia laughed as she and Lila went back to the truck.

"I'll guarantee this isn't over," Lila said once they were safely away from anyone overhearing them.

"Why did you step up like that?"

"Hey, you own this business. The last thing you need is getting involved in some petty catfight between the town harlot and part of the bridal party that has paid you to cater their event." Lila looked out the truck window. "This storm is just getting started."

It appeared that things had begun to settle down and roll into a pleasant groove as the guests stuffed their faces with Rusty's delicious burgers and fries. Presents were opened, and a million oohs and aahs could be heard as fancy cutlery and thick bathroom towels and all the other necessities that a newlywed couple needed to survive were unwrapped.

Looking at her watch, Amelia yawned. She and Lila had cleaned up the truck and made a list of what they'd need for Monday. While they were discussing the menu, a bleary-eyed Tabitha Miller approached the open window with her daughter by her side.

"Your cupcakes were wonderful," she said. A long strand of her red hair fell across her face, and she brushed it back into place.

"They really were," Darcy piped up. "We are going to tell everyone we know about them."

"Yes, everyone," Tabitha gushed, handing Amelia a check that was even more generous than the price they had agreed upon.

"Tabitha, I think you may have miscalculated. We had agreed on..."

"It's a tip. I saw your children when they stopped by here." She took her daughter's hand. "Before you know it, they'll be off with their own lives."

Amelia smiled, biting her tongue to keep her tears back.

"Come on, Mama. No more gushy stuff." Darcy looked at Amelia. "I have thugs and drunks calling me all kinds of names, taking swings at me, and I don't bat an eye. My mom gets all sappy and it's like Niagara Falls." She wiped the tears from her eyes, and both women laughed. Without another word, they turned and went back to say good-bye to their guests, who were slowly starting to trickle their way out of the Twisted Spoke.

As was common in Oregon, the weather had decided it was sunny enough. Gray clouds rode on a cool breeze to cover up the sun. All the ladies in their pretty dresses were now covering up with shawls and jackets.

The Crier had thrown on a long trench coat and was quickly shuffling away as The Smoker and Shorty were calling her name. Without responding, The Crier climbed into her car and sped away. Her friends quickly followed suit.

"Some of them really shouldn't be driving," Lila teased.

"I was just thinking that." Amelia laughed then looked down at the check. "Lila, I think you earned yourself a bonus. None of this would have happened if you hadn't, well, thrown me into the deep end, so to speak."

"Nope. Tabitha is right. Use it for the kids. I told you, I'm not in this for the money. I've got money." She grinned.

Amelia huffed and stuffed the check into the front pocket of her jeans.

"What about Rusty?"

"What about him?" Lila cooed, inspecting her fingernails as if the cure for cancer might be found on the tips of her red nails.

"Don't give me 'What about him?'" Amelia laughed. "I saw..."

Both women stopped speaking.

Everyone stood still, frozen by something they hadn't seen but heard, loudly.

The screaming started and seemed as if it would never stop.

# Chapter Six

"She's dead!" came the hysterical cries of an older woman wearing a Twisted Spoke T-shirt and an apron around her waist. "She's dead in there!"

Both Amelia and Lila went running toward the bar area, as did Rusty, who had been behind the bar, Darcy, her mother, and a handful of the remaining guests.

"Rita, what are you talking about?" Rusty yelled. "Haven't we had enough excitement for today without..."

She was pointing at the ladies' room door, her hand trembling madly and her eyes blank with horror.

No one moved. Over the speakers, George Thorogood was croaking "Bad to the Bone." Even Darcy, trained to handle emergencies and tragedies, stood stone still, as if she wasn't sure she was even at her bridal shower anymore.

Rusty slowly walked to the door, placing a thick hand on Rita's shoulder as he passed her. He pushed open the bathroom door, and Amelia watched him as his face went white.

"Call 9-1-1" was all he said.

Darcy, who had worn a lovely cream-colored skirt with high heels, snapped into police mode and stomped up to Rusty, ready to push past him and the door marked "Ladies."

"You're not going in there," he grumbled.

"I'm a cop and..."

"And you are off duty. You're not going in there."

It was obvious from Randy's demeanor that he had had more than his fair share of staring contests with police. Darcy, a well-off girl from the suburbs who had turned "Blue," was no match. Her mother took her by the hand, and within minutes, sirens could be heard quickly approaching.

"Who is it?" Lila whispered to Amelia.

"It's Dana Foster," Rusty stated.

Amelia looked at Lila with wide eyes and shook her head no.

The Twisted Spoke had shifted to a weird kind of slow motion only to rev up when the police and ambulance arrived. As if someone had poked a hornet's nest, people were swarming around, making phone calls, pointing, waving their arms, and talking fast to police.

A slow thaw took over from there just as the plain brown sedan Amelia had seen before pulled up. Detective Walishovsky and his partner Gus climbed out of the car and, with slow, deliberate steps, walked up to Rusty, shook his hand, and followed him toward the ladies' room door.

"You know what I just noticed?" Amelia said to Lila, who was sitting on the back step of the truck as they waited for their turns to talk with the detectives.

"What's that?" Lila sighed.

"No one is crying."

Lila looked around, and her eyebrows shot up on her forehead.

"Not a single person looks distraught over this except for poor Rita, who saw it, but even she isn't crying." Amelia scratched her head. "I know Dana had a reputation, but was she that despised?"

"I didn't like her because she was a punk, but I didn't know her family. And the rumors, well, if they are all true, then I can believe someone finally did her in."

"Lila!" Amelia gasped.

Shaking her head and shrugging her shoulders, Lila rolled her eyes.

"It's true."

Before Amelia could ask what Lila had heard that differed from what she had heard, Detective Dan Walishovsky sauntered up to them. He stopped for a second, looking at Amelia, then quickly turned his attention to Lila.

"Good afternoon, ladies." He sounded like he was starting a speech. "I'd like to talk to you both, if I could, for a few minutes."

"About what?" Lila joked.

"Really, Lila, do you think that's appropriate?" Amelia stammered. The presence of Detective Walishovsky made her nervous. Not in a suspect-trying-to-avert-the-law kind of way but in a strangely attracted kind of way. She didn't want to be attracted to the detective. At her age, she should just be focusing on her children and her business, right? Who had the time or energy for a love life? What was she thinking? A love life at her age was almost vulgar. Almost.

"I take it you knew the victim, Miss Bergman?"

"I think, Detective, you might be hard pressed to find anyone in this town who didn't know Dana Foster." She inspected her fingernails. "It'll be even harder for you to find someone who is going to miss her."

"Lila and I were here because we were hired to cater the dessert for Officer Darcy's bridal shower. We were outside all day. Neither one of us were out of each other's sight the whole time. This is really one for the books, isn't it, Detective?"

"What do you mean?" His tone was serious, but in his eyes, Amelia saw a smile.

"A murder at a police officer's party? Sounds like the beginning of a bad joke."

The detective nodded his head and smirked just as his partner was approaching. Amelia watched him, wondering what went on in his mind as he immersed himself in these grisly situations.

"Dan, I'm coming up with nothing." Eugene Gus was the younger and less experienced detective. Compared to Walishovsky, he was a pleasant and inviting fellow who was more like a car salesman than a detective. "The women still here claim they didn't see or hear anything coming from the bathroom. No one saw her go in. From the look of it, the victim didn't know what was happening until it was too late."

"Can I ask? What did happen?" Amelia's eyes bounced from one man to the other, but her body leaned back slightly, as if she didn't want to get any of their words on her for fear they might stain.

"She had her head smashed and throat slit. Nearly decapitated her," Eugene stated as if he had seen this happen a million times before. "Multiple stab wounds in the back. We won't know exactly how many until the coroner takes a look."

Amelia stood with her mouth hanging open.

"Her head was smashed and her throat was slit?" Lila gasped. "*And* she was stabbed?"

"My gosh." Amelia put her hand over her mouth. Sure, she was in the consensus that Dana was a mess, but you didn't have to carry a badge to know that to have your throat slit and be stabbed was a sign of an intimate relationship gone bad. What had Dana done that warranted this?

"I'll ask you ladies to keep the details to yourselves," Detective Walishovsky whispered. "This is going to be a mess in more ways than one."

"Why do you say that?" Amelia asked.

"Dana Foster comes from a wealthy family. These are always a mess."

Eugene leaned in to his partner, and Amelia overheard the words he whispered. They broke her heart in a way she never would have imagined.

"Do you want me to make the phone call to the parents, or do you want to do it?"

"I'll do it. They won't be able to get back to town for a few days. We can get her cleaned up by then."

Nodding his head, Eugene waved over the paramedics who, wearing latex gloves and rolling a stretcher, headed toward the ladies' bathroom.

"I'm sorry, Dan, that you have to make that phone call." Amelia comforted Detective Walishovsky and placed her hand on his arm. Calling him by his first name instead of "Detective" seemed the right thing to do, but she couldn't deny it made her feel tingles up her spine. Tears wanted to well in her eyes as she thought of being a mother and getting a call like that. It tore at her heart. Biting her tongue, she kept the tears back.

He nodded and squeezed her hand, holding on to it for a moment.

"I like your haircut." Again, his face didn't move, but his eyes smiled after he finally released her hand. Amelia blushed and patted the back of her neck.

"Th-thanks. It's easier to take care of," she stuttered. Here there was a dead girl just a few feet away from her and she was going on about her hair. She sounded like a jerk.

"Not many women are pretty enough to get away with a haircut like that. It suits you."

Amelia's cheeks pushed up into her eyes as she grinned. That was just what she wanted to hear.

"I'm sure I'll have questions for you later, Amelia. I'll be in touch." He gave her a quick two-fingered salute as he headed back to his car to retrieve the radio and call in to dispatch at the station.

Nodding and folding her arms around herself, Amelia turned around to see Lila watching her.

"He's right. Your haircut does suit you."

"Oh, you are too much, Lila. Let's get out of here. We have one day off tomorrow, and I want to enjoy it. I don't think I'll go anywhere near my oven."

The two ladies drove out of the lot of the Twisted Spoke and headed home. First stop was Lila's apartment building and then her own two-bedroom home.

Just as Amelia set foot in her quiet, empty house, her phone rang.

It was Detective Walishovsky.

# Chapter Seven

"You want me to what?" Amelia stared straight ahead, holding the cell phone to her ear.

"I've got to go on a stakeout, and I was wondering if you wanted to come with me." He cleared his throat.

"Are you allowed to do that? I mean, have a civilian along with you while you are, you know, staking out?"

"I'm not asking you to interrogate a suspect or carry a weapon," he quipped. "You'll just be sitting in a car with me, a couple of sub sandwiches from Moody's, and some hot coffee. That's all."

"Subs from Moody's?" One of Amelia's favorite guilty pleasures was the delicious

Italian submarine sandwich from Moody's Restaurant. Detective Walishovsky knew how to tempt her. Still, she was suspicious of his intent.

"Okay, I'm in," Amelia finally replied.

"Good, I'll pick you up in an hour."

"Detective, can I ask why?"

She heard Walishovsky clear his throat again.

"I'd like to discuss something with you, but not over the phone."

He said nothing more.

"Oh, well, okay, then."

After hanging up the phone, Amelia went upstairs for a quick shower and a change of clothes. While the hot water wiped the grime of the afternoon's gory event off her skin, she wondered what the detective had on his mind.

*Maybe he's interested in me?* Immediately Amelia's cheeks turned red, and she gasped. Who said that? Why would such a thought cross her mind? No. No. No. With considerable effort, she pushed the thought out of her head.

"What does one wear to a stakeout?" she mused loudly. That ought to show those crazy romantic thoughts who was in charge. "Something comfortable." Pulling out an old pair of jeans and a baggy T-shirt, she stood in front of the full-length mirror attached to her closet and squinted.

"You look like an Oompa-Loompa, Amelia," she scolded. "There is nothing wrong with looking like a lady."

After trying two pairs of slacks, a long skirt, and a muumuu, she found a pair of plain black running pants that she never ran in and an oversized flannel shirt, just what she was looking for.

"Comfy, and if I get food on my shirt, no one will notice." She nodded her head at her reflection just as the doorbell rang. Quickly glancing at her hair, she was happy to see it still looked nice. Quietly making her way down the steps, she pulled open the door to find Detective Walishovsky wearing the same jacket, loosened tie, and hard shoes he had worn at the Twisted Spoke earlier today.

"Hi, Detective." Amelia smiled, stepping aside for him to come in.

"Please, call me Dan," he said, stooping slightly to enter the front door. "Detective Walishovsky is a mouthful."

"Come on in, Dan." She chuckled. "Just give me a second and I'll be ready." She went to the freezer, grabbed a bag of individually wrapped brownies, and stuffed them in her purse. "Can't forget dessert."

"Not with the woman who owns the Pink Cupcake." He smirked, holding the door for her.

*This isn't a date*, Amelia repeated in her head. *This isn't a date, so just be yourself. Just be blunt. Ask lots of questions. That's it. Questions.*

"I'm sorry, Dan, I don't mean to be pushy, but can you tell me what this is all about?" She nervously pulled at the cuffs of her sleeves while Dan drove. "When the detective of a murder case asks you to join him on a stakeout, it sounds like the beginning of a crime story, don't you think?"

"It sort of is."

"Am I a suspect?"

"Not yet," he joked, making Amelia stop and stare before she realized he was kidding.

"You've got a look that makes me wonder when you're joking and when you're not." Amelia rolled her eyes at him. "I get the feeling that cop humor is a lot different from civilian humor, too."

"You're probably right." Just as they pulled into Moody's parking lot, a bubbly teenager about eighteen years old came strutting out of the restaurant with a large brown bag and a cup holder with two large, steaming cups balancing in it.

"Here you go, Detective," she gushed while handing him the food.

"Thank you, Amy," Dan grumbled, barely cracking a smile as he handed her money for the food.

"If you'll hold on, I'll get you your change."

"Just keep it, honey."

"Thanks, Detective." Tilting her head to the right, she waved good-bye. "Be careful out there."

"I will."

Handing everything over to Amelia to hold, Dan drove out of the parking lot and headed south on Brightway Road.

"Well, she sure likes you," Amelia teased.

"I've been getting sandwiches there for years. Amy is a good kid I arrested once."

"Really?" Amelia shook her head.

"Yeah, you know the story. A young girl not getting enough attention at home. Whatever. So, I picked her up for panhandling. She was rough around the edges."

Amelia was mesmerized.

"She smoked, drank, slept in the park sometimes." Dan scratched his chin. "Her parents had a nice home, but a nice home wasn't what she needed. Frankly, what she needed was a swift kick in the behind."

"Most teenagers do." Amelia nodded her head.

"Yeah, so I picked her up for panhandling. She had never been arrested before. It wasn't like what she saw in the movies or even on television shows. She's a cute girl with long hair. They'll put you in the infirmary for that."

"Really?"

"Oh, yeah." Dan nodded as he looked at the numbers on the row of buildings they were slowly cruising past. "So, she gets thrown in with the other women that had been picked up that night. Let me tell you, I was scared of some of them."

Shaking her head, Amelia stared at the detective, completely engrossed in the tale.

"Hookers, drunks, drug addicts. That particular night there were about twelve other women in the holding cell. Amy was the youngest and the greenest. They swooped down on her like gulls on a crab."

"My gosh!"

"So, I hear all this commotion and go take a look. Amy is in the corner with a drunk woman at least four times bigger than her screaming in her face and threatening her. Amy's crying and trying to be tough." He shook his head. "I could have let her stay in there, but something just wouldn't let me."

Amelia nodded eagerly, waiting for the rest of the story.

"So I got a couple of female cops to get her out of there. She was sixteen at the time. I took her to my desk, and we had a talk."

"What did she say?"

"You can always tell the teenagers that don't want to be bad. They have no secrets. They'll tell you anything and everything about themselves." He rolled his eyes. "She told me about her parents. Her boyfriend. School. What she wanted to be when she grew up. What she hated. What her favorite color was. She went on and on."

Amelia chortled, thinking of Meg and her best friend, Katherine, who fit this description to a tee.

"Finally I told her that if she could communicate this well with me, she should have no problem talking to her parents or her teachers. She was no dummy. She was just a kid."

"So what happened?"

"Well, I told her that her parents were gonna be pissed when they came to pick her up. And they were. But I said if she needed help that I'd be happy to find her someone who wouldn't turn her away." He looked down at his coffee. "Would you mind fixing the lid on that for me?"

Amelia bent back the lip of the lid so the bitter aroma of the brew filled the car. Dan removed it from the cardboard holder, took a sip, and handed it back to Amelia.

"About a week later, she came into the station looking for me. She had had a fight with her boyfriend. Her parents wouldn't listen, and she was losing her mind." He took a deep breath. "I introduced her to Officer Claire Higgens, who was just one of those people that was good with kids."

"What did she do?"

"Claire did what she always does. She just listened." Dan clicked his tongue. "It was all she needed. Amy left that night, then came back with her mother, and they had a card for me and flowers for Claire."

"That was sweet." Amelia was still spellbound by the story.

"Yes, she said she broke up with her boyfriend. She broke away from the kids she was hanging out with and decided she wanted to be a cop."

"Well, isn't that something?"

Again, Dan shook his head. There was a hint of pride on his face, but it was carefully guarded. It was like he didn't want anyone to think he did something nice for fear it might ruin his reputation as a hardened detective.

"So, she's nineteen now and taking classes at the community college to save money. The girl has been working at Moody's for three years and has saved almost every penny. She could have gotten a scholarship, but her grades weren't high enough for long enough. You know those snobby schools expects As from third grade on."

Laughing, Amelia thought of her ex-husband, who placed a good bit of value on his degree from UCLA. He'd hate Dan. Perhaps that was a secret, deep-down reason Amelia found the detective so fascinating.

"But she's doing it. When things get hard, she just weathers the storm, tells me or Officer Higgens about it, and moves on. More adults should have her perspective."

"I agree." Amelia was enjoying herself.

"She's worked every weekend and from three p.m. until nine p.m. twice a week. I see her all the time because I eat here so much."

Dan patted his stomach, which appeared to be as flat as a board from where Amelia was sitting.

"That is an amazing story. Hey, where are we?" Amelia looked out her window and didn't recognize the scenery. There was an empty construction site on her left and a couple of trailers on her right plus warehouses as far as she could see down the block. The whole area looked like some postapocalyptic wasteland.

"See those trailers over there?" Dan indicated with his eyes what he was talking about.

Amelia nodded.

"There's a guy who uses that for business that isn't exactly legal. We're keeping tabs on who's coming and going."

"What if nobody comes or goes?"

"Then we only have two hours' worth of paperwork to do."

"And if you do see someone of interest?"

"That will be four hours of paperwork."

Dan drove the sedan around the block to a stretch of street that had a perfect view of the trailers but was hidden from them by tall weeds and a chain-link fence.

Cutting off the engine, Dan radioed in to the station where he was, then pulled out the sandwiches, handing one to Amelia and keeping the other for himself.

"Dinner is served."

"How did you know I liked the Italian sub?"

"I've tasted your cupcakes. The Italian subs are the best thing on the menu. I thought it was a pretty safe bet that you'd like the tastiest thing they make." Dan took a big bite and gave Amelia a wink.

Smiling, she took a bite then wiped her mouth with a napkin.

"So, what did you want to talk about?"

Swallowing hard, Dan took a sip of coffee, keeping his eyes on the trailer across the street.

"Dana Foster."

"I don't know her. I only know of her," Amelia said in between bites. She retold her tale of nearly being run off the road just the other day. "But that is really the only contact I've ever had with the girl."

"But you know stories about her?"

"Just what I've heard around town. She had always been like the elusive snipe. People would talk about her and all her shenanigans, but I never witnessed anything other than her trying to run me off the road." Amelia chewed slowly, enjoying the food and the company.

"Can you tell me what you've heard?"

"Dana is probably the rich version of your little friend Amy." Amelia carefully pulled the tab off her coffee top and took a sip. "Except she never got that kick in the pants."

Dan nodded with his mouth full of food.

"I heard she stole a few boyfriends and was in the police blotter every once in a while. I never heard of anything that would warrant someone killing her."

Still staring ahead at the motionless trailer, Dan listened but said nothing.

"I'm sorry. I guess you brought me out here for a whole lot of nothing."

Dan looked at Amelia then shook his head no.

"Are you kidding?" He wiped his mouth on the back of his hand. "Have you ever talked to my partner? He's a good kid, but he's exactly that, a kid. Sometimes it's nice to just vent to someone your own age."

Amelia relaxed and continued eating her sandwich as Dan told her a little more about the guy they were watching.

"How long do we have to stay?" Amelia asked, squinting at the trailer.

"Did you see that blue Ford pull out as we arrived?" Dan reached underneath his seat and pulled out a set of binoculars. He brought them up to his eyes and adjusted the focus.

"No."

"That's right. Because Detective Ross had been watching for the day shift. You and I watch for another two or three hours, if that's okay."

"I've got no plans." Amelia reached out her hand for the binoculars.

Without skipping a beat, Dan handed them over. While Amelia was busy studying the trailer, she didn't notice Detective Dan Walishovsky studying her. He couldn't help it. He thought she was pretty.

For the following three hours, they talked. Amelia couldn't help bragging on her children. She spoke about Lila and how the Pink Cupcake came into existence. That reminded her she had brought brownies for dessert.

"These are almost as good as your cupcakes," Dan mumbled with his mouth full.

"Almost?"

"There is something about those orange-ginger things you make that keep a man up at night."

"Detective, really?" She rolled her eyes. "Those are my special Orange Blossoms. I actually use lemon cake with fresh ginger and vanilla and orange extract mixed together. The frosting is plain vanilla with orange extract added. Pretty simple, right?"

"They're delicious."

"Well, I'll be sure to bake you a batch for your birthday or Christmas or..."

"Or both." He chuckled at his own joke and peered through the binoculars again. "Wait, what is this?"

Amelia froze and stared in the direction of the trailer.

"What is it?" she whispered. "Who are those people?"

"That looks like Mick O'Donell and his business partner's wife."

Amelia clapped her hand over her mouth. She had no idea who Mick O'Donell was or who his business partner was, but she knew being with his wife was probably not a good thing.

Reaching underneath his seat, Dan pulled out a camera and began snapping pictures of the two people exiting the trailer. They briefly kissed, and it was not the kiss of two friends who'd spent the late afternoon sipping coffee.

"Okay." Dan breathed. "I think we can call it a night."

"What else have you got underneath your seat?" Amelia asked.

"I think there's a slim jim, lockpick set, evidence bags, rubber gloves. You know, the usual."

As Dan drove Amelia home, they began to talk about the Dana Foster murder again.

"Don't murders that violent indicate the victim knew the attacker?" Amelia inquired. "That's what I hear on all the crime shows."

"Usually. I think in Dana's case that it will probably turn out to be some jealous boyfriend or an ex-boyfriend. I'd bet my reputation on it."

"But she was with a bunch of women at the party. And from what I saw when she arrived, there wasn't a friend of hers among the entire group."

"Women usually don't kill, and when they do, messy isn't usually their style. Like that teenager who tried to kill the wife of her much older boyfriend. She took a shot at her when she answered the front door. Guns put a distance between the killer and the victim. In their heads, they are not getting as 'dirty' even though the result is the same whether they used a knife, chainsaw, ice pick, whatever."

"But no one was watching all the women all at once. One could have snuck off and…"

"You also forget that quite a few of those women were police officers, or relatives of police officers. Do you really think they'd do something so risky?"

Amelia wondered if Dan had considered any of the policewomen at the party as real suspects or if they automatically got a pass because they were police officers.

"I think people screw up good things all the time." John popped into her head, but she quickly pushed him aside.

"No. The autopsy should be just about done. I'll have more information once I read that. But dollars to doughnuts, it's an ex."

Looking out the window, Amelia watched the scenery become more and more familiar as Dan drove.

"You don't think you're maybe just a little biased about who the suspects might be?" The words ran out of her mouth and left a bitter taste behind. *What are you doing? He's been completely nice all night, right? Why jump down his throat?* She bit her lip and looked at Dan. His face seemed to darken with shadows as his eyebrows creased in the middle.

"After all the years I've been on the force, I just know what to look for." He looked at

Amelia as if he were laying out evidence in front of her that proved she was a jerk. "You can't learn what I know by watching television."

Clearing her throat, Amelia fidgeted with the cuff of her shirt again.

"I didn't mean anything by it. I was just..."

"You were just voicing a suspicion that most of the public has these days about cops. That we cover for one another." His voice was cool, low, but very agitated. "No matter what the crime."

"No. That isn't what I meant."

"Sure it is." He took a deep breath. "It's tough being the good guy when bad guys wear the same clothes, but that isn't me. And it isn't anyone in my department."

"Dan, I certainly didn't mean to..."

"You're down this street, right?"

Looking at the detective's face, Amelia was sure she saw a genuine hurt there.

"Yeah. Just down two blocks and take a left. You'll see the truck at the end of the street."

As they were pulling into the driveway, Amelia gathered up the empty food wrappers and containers to throw away in her trashcan. Taking a deep breath, she opened the door and stepped out. But before closing the door, she leaned down.

"Thanks for taking me along. I really had a good time. It was better than any movie that's out there." She smiled, hoping to get a reaction, but instead just got a couple of nods and what looked like a very forced grimace.

"Have a good night, Amelia." Dan's voice was low, as if he were talking to a child. It made Amelia think of John and all the times he'd sulked, knowing full well that she was right about something but refusing to give her even that small victory.

"Okay, maybe you are right. Maybe I did think you were willing to protect your friends first. I know if it were one of my children in this kind of trouble, I'd turn over ever rock, every leaf, every clue to prove it wasn't them." She swallowed. "And only then, when I was sure of the ugly truth, would I hand them over. That doesn't make me a bad guy." Standing up straight, she slammed the car door and walked up to the front door. Only once she was inside and the front door was shut and locked did Dan finally pull away.

"Everyone is always so touchy," she mumbled, rubbing her arms as she went upstairs. In the quiet of the house, she got ready for bed and wondered about Dana Foster.

With her entire Sunday free, Amelia thought it might be a good day to do a little snooping, starting with Tabitha Miller, the mother of the bride at the party.

# Chapter Eight

"What a pleasant surprise," Tabitha said when she opened her front door to see Amelia standing there. Her eyes were clear and sparkly, and her makeup, although perfectly applied already at 9:00 a.m., was lighter and made her look at least ten years younger that the heavy paint she had been wearing the previous day. "Please come in."

"I'm sorry to call on you so early, Tabitha."

"It's no trouble. We're early risers here. Is there a problem with the check or..."

"No. No. Nothing like that." Amelia followed Tabitha into the kitchen. It was a beautiful red-bricked room with stainless steel appliances and an island in the middle with four barstools placed around it. The fridge was covered with pictures of Darcy and Mr. Miller and grocery lists, a calendar with days circled, and other reminders. "I was hoping I could talk to you about Dana Foster."

"What a mess." Tabitha shook her head while pulling down two coffee cups. "Cream or sugar?"

"Black is fine. Thanks."

"I first heard of Dana Foster when Darcy was a freshman at the academy," she said while pouring coffee for both of them.

Tabitha went on to explain that Dana had been wild from the get-go. Her parents lived in an even nicer area of Sarkis Estates, her father having some government ties and her mother being extremely successful in real estate, selling million-dollar homes on the waterfront and in downtown Portland.

"She was only sixteen and was at some party. She and another girl got into an argument. Dana drove the girl's new Jeep off a pier. Just put it in drive and let it go."

"Well, there had to have been consequences, right?" Amelia was pretty sure she already knew the answer.

"Yeah, for her father, who wrote a check and headed off to the golf course."

Amelia's eyes bugged, and she took a sip of coffee.

"Is that the only thing?"

"No." Tabitha shook her head. "There were other things. There were lots of stories that included men. Boyfriends and other girls' boyfriends and even some husbands."

"Really?"

"The stories with the boys, I can believe because you know how dumb young people can be when they are in love. But there are some people out there who will testify under oath that they know Dana had more than one man paying her bills, buying her clothes, and I just don't know if I believe those."

"Why? What makes you doubt them?"

"Well, Dana's uncle owns the Twisted Spoke. Now, that place is great. You met Rusty, and before the...*murder*"—Tabitha whispered the word—"everything is fine, the food is great, drinks aren't too expensive. But at night, a pretty rough element shows up there. Well, you can bet that Dana slipped right in."

Amelia nodded and took a sip.

"Some of those bikers are just weekend warriors. You know, the kind of guys who pay thousands of dollars for a motorcycle and ride it when the weather is nice on weekends, just to be seen." Tabitha shook her head. "Then you have those people who live that lifestyle. They ride their bikes in any kind of weather, work hard jobs, maybe, or maybe don't have anything higher than a high-school education."

"Sure." Amelia thought of Rusty, who was obviously a real biker but the manager of a restaurant as well.

"And then there are those people that survive on the road. They have ways of making money, and it's all in cash. They don't necessarily sleep indoors unless you want to count the time they've done in prison. They live differently than you and me. A *lot* differently."

"Did Dana hang with this crowd?"

"From what I heard, she really just flitted around the fringe. To be a biker's woman is no different than joining a gang in the city. One man's 'old lady' belongs to the group, if you catch my meaning. You party hard and find ways to scrape by, and those ways aren't usually safe. Dana had a Corvette. She had a cell phone. She had credit cards.

She wasn't going to give all that up to live off the back of a bike. But I think she liked to slum it with them."

"Do you think she made one of them mad and they did this to her?"

Tabitha thought for a moment and rapped her manicured red nails on the counter.

"I think it is more likely than not."

Amelia took another sip of her coffee.

"Tell me, Tabitha, how is it that you know so much about this? I feel I've gotten a real education today."

"You forget, Amelia, my daughter is a police officer. I've read up on anything and everything going on in various crime worlds, so I know what my daughter is doing. Thankfully she is mostly pulling over speeders and locking up drunks." Tabitha's eyes began to water. "But we never stop being parents. I want her to be able to talk to me if things ever get too serious. And that meant toughening up about some of the seedier things in life."

"She's lucky to have you, Tabitha."

The two women talked for a few more minutes before Amelia said her good-byes and left the Miller home. As she drove, she thought about the world of bikers and thought she might just pay a visit to Rusty at the Twisted Spoke.

# Chapter Nine

"How's that friend of yours, Miss Bergman?" Rusty asked Amelia as he scooted behind the bar of the empty restaurant.

The Twisted Spoke had been shut down while the police investigated the crime scene that was the ladies' room. Then it remained closed while the hazmat team had to come and clean up the blood.

"She's fine, Rusty. I'll tell her you asked," Amelia replied, pulling up a stool.

Rusty's smile was tired.

"Just a Coke. Keep the good stuff for the regulars. When do you get to open up again?"

"They said in another twenty-four to forty-eight hours."

"That's not too bad." Amelia tried to sound cheery.

"Considering the alternative would be to close down altogether. Yeah, another two days won't kill us. Poor choice of words." He let out a deep breath as he pressed the button for Coke on the head of the nozzle that squirted water, seltzer, Coke and 7UP.

"So, I hate to bother you at this difficult time but..."

"It's not difficult. Not for me. Except that I'm going out of my gourd without work to do." Rusty ruffled as he spoke. "That girl was nothing but trouble. Even when she's dead, she's got everything and everyone in a tizzy."

"Well, I don't think she planned it." Amelia took a sip of her Coke and watched for Rusty's response.

"To be honest, I'm surprised she made it to the age of twenty."

Amelia pursed her lips and shook her head, shrugging her shoulders.

"Why would you say that?"

"Miss Amelia, that girl was just bad news all around. She didn't have a kind bone in her body."

Rusty's blatant honesty was surprisingly refreshing.

"You see, there are young people who are spoiled and throw tantrums and fits, pouting and sulking when they don't get their way. But Dana, she was different. If she didn't get her way, she didn't just sulk around. She got revenge."

"What do you mean?"

Rusty cracked his knuckles and leaned on the bar.

"Well, let me just say that there are a few broken relationships and a few broken homes due to Dana Foster's bruised ego."

Amelia's eyes widened.

"Oh, yeah." Rusty continued, leaning in closer. "You know, her uncle owns this place. That is the only reason she had a job here. She barely waited tables, didn't clean or cook. She managed to drink a good bit of the booze. Let's face facts. She was more than a little good-looking. The men were never in short supply when she was on the roster to work."

Amelia watched Rusty shake his head.

"It makes me queasy to even say it out loud, but there was a little more going on between her and her uncle."

Amelia gasped.

"You can't be serious." She put her hand up to her lips.

"I am one hundred percent serious. And the crazy thing is that Jack, her uncle, was a jealous man. He hires her to work at his biker bar. Then, he blows his top every couple of nights because some Hell's Angels wannabe has her sittin' on his lap."

Rusty went on to explain that a good number of the fights in the Twisted Spoke were a result of the uncle's jealousy.

"So are you saying they...you know..." Amelia cupped her hands as if she were rubbing a crystal ball.

"I ain't sayin' they did that. But I ain't sayin' they didn't. All I know is that I have a couple of nieces, and it would be a cold day in hell before I brought them to this place on a Friday or Saturday night. I also wouldn't slap them on their backsides, or slow dance with them, or pull them aside to whisper to them in the dark corners of this place. Call me crazy, but I just wouldn't do that."

"Did you ever say anything to him?"

"No. I'm just the manager of this place. But I did witness his wife step up to the plate and give Dana a good tongue lashing."

"And what did that do?"

"Are you kidding? It just turned up the heat. That girl found every opportunity to put her hands on the man. And he was lovin' it, too."

"But you don't think Dana's aunt would kill her, do you?"

"Her name is Cindy. Cindy's no stranger to the streets. She has her own bike. She and Jack met at Daytona Bike Week almost two decades ago. Cindy certainly wasn't and isn't some babe in the woods. If she wanted to get ugly, she knows how. And if she didn't kill Dana herself, she certainly knew of people who were more than willing to do some dirty work for a few dollars."

"What about Jack? Could he have gotten jealous enough to, you know?" She nodded her head toward the ladies' room.

"Oh, I wouldn't put it past him at all," Randy scoffed. "Dana had him wrapped around her finger."

"So if all that is true, why isn't he here?"

"He and Cindy are in Malibu. It's their anniversary." Rusty rubbed his stubbly chin, giving off the sound of scratching sandpaper.

"Well, that's a pretty good alibi," Amelia muttered.

A few moments of quiet passed between them before Amelia spoke up again.

"What about the women that were at the bridal shower when it happened? Do you think any of them had anything to do with it?"

Rusty shrugged, pulling the corners of his lips down.

"A few of them lost their boyfriends to Dana. She collected men like some people collect stamps. She'd fuss and fawn over them until they finally gave in to the temptation. Then she'd stick them in a tight place where they'd be gawked and stared at. It amused her to see women upset."

He turned and opened a cooler to pull out a bottle of water. He twisted off the cap, took a gulp, then set the bottle down.

"My waitress, Rita, stumbled across the body first. She is just a sweetheart. Always on time. Never sick. Well, not long ago her daughter got pregnant. She and her husband apparently had been trying for some time. So the girl got pregnant, but something happened where she lost the baby."

"Oh, how sad." Amelia had had a close call with Adam when she was in her third month of carrying him. She had never prayed to God as hard as she had at that time for him to be okay. She couldn't imagine the sadness and disappointment Rita's daughter must have felt.

"Well, Dana, in her infinite wisdom, made light of it. Now, I'm just an old redneck, but there are certain things that just aren't joke appropriate. Vietnam is one. And babies passing is another." He said this through tightly held lips. It was as if he were reliving the incident and it made him angrier and angrier. "That witch said something about the baby being ugly or brain damaged or some other cruel assumption. Well, that sweetheart named Rita nearly tore Dana's head off. Had Jack not stepped in, I think Rita would have put Dana in the hospital, but not before she lost a few clumps of that hair of hers."

"But I saw Rita," Amelia protested. "She didn't look strong enough to choke a kitten."

"I don't think she's a suspect, but I do know that she has a couple of Chicago mobsters as close cousins. Real kneecap breakers, you know?" Rusty took Amelia's glass and held it under the nozzle, giving her a refill. "I'm not saying she did anything any more than Jack or Cindy did. I'm just saying that Dana had more enemies than friends. The police are going to have a hard time narrowing down who had the strongest motive."

Amelia thanked him for the refill then swiveled in her seat.

"What about you, Rusty? Did she put on any shenanigans with you?"

"Oh, she tried, but nothing stuck." Rusty smiled as if he were proud of himself. "I've learned over the years that a pretty face comes a dime a dozen. I've got a more distinguished palate." He winked, the right side of his face crinkling into happy wrinkles.

"I'll bet you do. Thanks for your time, Rusty." Amelia smiled. "On that note, I'll make sure I tell Lila you'll be back up and running in the next day or two."

"You do that."

Rusty shook Amelia's hand, and she left the Twisted Spoke feeling nowhere nearer any answer as to who might have done this to Dana. But she sure was getting an education about the woman and her lifestyle, if that's what you'd call it.

It wasn't until she was handling the midmorning rush that she got a break.

# Chapter Ten

"I might go pay Rusty a visit," Lila chirped while adding one fresh Bing cherry to the fourth batch of coconut cherry cupcakes that were flying out of the truck and into the hands of the long line of customers.

"Well, I've seen twitterpated, and that boy is under your spell, for sure."

Lila laughed but shook her head.

"I'm not sure how to let him down easy. I'm just not interested." She shrugged her shoulders. "I've got too many other things on my mind. Plus, as a very active staff member of the Pink Cupcake, I really can't jeopardize my position with such a distraction."

"Oh, you're going to break his heart." Amelia sighed.

"He'll get over it."

It was a noisy, giggling group of women appearing in the window that made both Amelia and Lila freeze and stare.

"Remember us?" came the singsongy voice of a woman with long hair and heavy mascara.

Both Amelia and Lila stared.

"The shower? You brought those delicious cupcakes?"

Like a slap across the face, Amelia recognized The Crier, her friend The Smoker, and next to her, down a few inches, was Shorty.

"Oh, yes, hello, girls." Amelia grinned and leaned on the counter.

"Your cupcakes are addictive. We've walked all the way from State Street." The Crier teetered.

"In heels," Shorty added.

"Well, I appreciate that," Amelia replied. "That was some shower, right?" Amelia studied their reactions.

"Oh my gosh!" gushed Shorty. "We couldn't believe it. I mean, truthfully, no one liked Dana. But to kill her?"

"And with a knife?" The Smoker added. "I've heard that that makes it a crime of passion because it's so intimate. You gotta get close to someone to do that."

The girls continued clucking away except The Crier. She checked her watch, shifted from foot to foot, and finally put one hand to her stomach and the other on her head.

"You guys, we need to get going," she whined as she hurriedly handed her credit card to Amelia to pay for all three treats.

Like someone had thrown a bucket of water on the scene, both girls stopped and looked at their friend. Something was silently communicated between all three of them, and before Amelia could ask, they ordered three coconut cherry cupcakes, paid in full, and waved as they quickly hobbled in their heels through the grass and out of sight.

Amelia looked down at the credit card receipt. The Crier's name was Francine McManahan.

After another day in the black, Amelia and Lila shut down for the day. Looking at her phone, Amelia didn't have any messages from her kids, her ex, or Detective Walishovsky. She had thought that maybe he'd have called to say sorry for overreacting on Saturday, but no such luck.

Arriving home, she stepped into the house and could smell something cooking.

"Hey!" she shouted. "What's cooking?"

"Hi, Mom," Meg and Adam answered in unison. "We're making vegetable fried rice."

"Yum!" Amelia rubbed her stomach as she walked into the kitchen. It looked as if a bomb had gone off, as it usually did when the kids cooked. Adam's laptop was perched in a corner of the counter, playing some strange music that they both knew all the words to. It was like a foreign language to Amelia, but she smiled all the same.

How terrible it must be for the Fosters. They were coming home from some exotic place to bury their only daughter. Watching Meg dance around as she stirred the rice, bumping her brother with her hip and calling him things like spaz and nerd, made Amelia want to burst into tears and hug them both. But she didn't.

"It smells really good. I'm starved."

"How'd you do today?" Adam asked. "Did we make a million dollars yet?"

"Not yet. But we're getting there. How were things at your father's?"

Both kids became quiet and gave each other knowing glances.

"I don't have to smoke a pipe and wear a deerstalker hat to deduce something is afoot," Amelia replied. She watched as her children stopped what they were doing and stood still. Meg looked at her big brother.

"Dad moved Jennifer into the house." He sighed, thrusting his hands into his pockets. Meg looked down and sniffled.

"Okay." Amelia felt as if she had just been punched but furrowed her eyebrows, tilted her head, and looked at her children. "And this bothers you guys?"

"It's just that if she's moving in, that means you and Dad are officially over." Adam stepped up behind his sister, who was slowly stirring the rice and sniffled again.

"You guys, your dad and I have been officially over for a while." Amelia set down her purse and walked over to them. "But where you both are concerned, we've agreed we'll never be over. We love you both so much."

"Jennifer said they were talking about marriage and babies."

*Of course they were.* Amelia shook her head and bit her tongue to make sure the disgust didn't show on her face.

"Well, your dad is moving on. Just like we have, right? We've got the Pink Cupcake, and Adam, you're basically running my public relations all by yourself. Meg, it won't be long before you're working alongside me for an actual paycheck." She took a deep breath and held it for a second.

"I know you might feel bad or confused or funny about the whole thing"—she smoothed Meg's hair gently—"but remember, your dad and I will always love you both."

"Even if they have a new baby?" Meg chirped. Her eyes were red.

"Well, look, they haven't even had a wedding or anything yet. At least not that we know of." Amelia mumbled that last part. "Let's not worry about what hasn't happened yet. Okay? Besides, all this heart-to-heart stuff has postponed dinner, and I'm starving."

The kids cheered up as they continued to cook dinner. Amelia went upstairs to wash up and change clothes. Just as she was washing her face, her cell phone went off in her pocket.

"Hi, Amelia."

"Hi, John." She patted the back of her head, enjoying the feel of her short cut. "The kids were just talking about you."

"So you've heard?"

"Look, if it's about you and Jennifer getting married and having babies, I couldn't be happ..."

"Married? Babies? Where is this coming from?"

"From the kids. They said Jennifer had moved in with you and you're talking about marriage and babies. Look, I couldn't be happier for you, really. Just don't forget about them, okay?"

"Jennifer has moved in, yes." John's voice was firm, and it brought back memories that Amelia didn't like. The condescending comments about her family, her education, and a dozen other nitpicks flooded over her, and she found herself involuntarily squeezing the telephone receiver tightly. "But we haven't discussed getting married. I mean, not in any real depth."

"That's between you and her. But John, Adam told me you were talking about throwing him a party at some hotel downtown. I'm telling you now that you can't do that."

"Well, Amelia, Jennifer and I thought it would be nice to throw him a party..."

"At a hotel? Do you know how irresponsible teenagers are?"

"We're talking about Adam, not just some kid down the street." John chuckled as if Amelia had said something humorous.

"Yes, your sixteen-year-old son. I'm raising him. I know who he is and how great he is, and I want to keep him that way. John, he doesn't need a big party for turning a year older."

"Jennifer said she had a great time when her father threw her a fancy party for her seventeenth birthday, and I just thought..."

"You can't be serious," Amelia barked. "Do you realize she had her seventeenth birthday just eight years ago? I'm telling you now, Adam is not getting some extravagant party so you can feel like a cool dad who sees them on the weekends."

"Are you going to be the one who breaks it to him?"

"If I have to." Amelia rubbed her head. "Look, I just got home from work, and I'm tired. We can discuss this later. But John, if you go ahead with this after I've made my feelings perfectly clear, we are going to have problems that neither one of us need. Please, don't make this about you and your ego."

"If I have the money to throw my son a party, I will," John spat. "I've asked you for favors, too, and you completely ignored them."

"What have you ever asked me to do for the kids that I ever ignored?"

"Not for the kids but for me."

"Well, that is why I *don't* do them. *You* don't need me anymore, John. But the kids do. They need us both, and they need us to work together. You and me. Not you, Jennifer, and me. Just you and me."

John let out a frustrated sigh on the other end of the phone. Amelia knew the conversation was done, and she was glad for it.

"I'll think about it" was all he said.

"Thanks, John."

"I heard there was some kind of accident at the place you were having that party at?" Amelia could tell by John's voice he was going to take a jab. She braced herself.

"Yeah, that was something. We were long gone before it happened," she lied. The coverage on the news was surprisingly brief, and thankfully, there was no shot of the Pink Cupcake truck in any of the footage.

"That's the job you want Meg, your four-teen-year-old daughter, working at? The one your son is constantly posting things online for?" His voice had razor-sharp barbs around every word. "But a supervised party downtown is out of the question?"

"That isn't fair, John." Amelia was getting angrier by the minute.

"Of course it isn't. It's all about what you think is best. Well, I think Adam deserves a party like all the other kids have."

Amelia rolled her eyes up to the ceiling and wondered what other kids his age were having parties in hotels in the heart of the city. Certainly none of the kids he associated with.

"John, I'm not arguing with you. You know how I feel. Now, I'm going downstairs to have a nice meal that your children prepared for me. Good-bye, John."

He was still saying something as Amelia hung up the phone. He rang her back, but she silenced her ringtone and left the device on her bed as she went downstairs. If John had seen the news about Dana Foster on television, why didn't he see how precious life was and how things could change for the worse in a matter of seconds? Instead he insisted on arguing over parties and his girlfriend's crazy ideas.

"I hope the table is set because I'm hungry," she yelled down the stairs as she approached.

"Come on, Mom. We're just about done," Meg replied.

That night, they ate dinner together in the tiny kitchen. Meg talked about her friend Katherine and some girls and some boys and teachers and a million other things in her life, all in the span of about five minutes. Adam ate pensively and only spoke to add a joke or tease his sister. It was a lovely time.

Amelia offered to clean the kitchen for the kids in return for such a nice spread.

She thought they were getting so big so fast.

Maybe Adam should have a fancy party. He wasn't that adorable little boy who would hang on her side and hold her hand in the parking lot anymore. He was almost a man. Heck, in some cultures he was a man. She couldn't decide what to do for his birthday that was still five months away.

Instead, Amelia wondered about Dana Foster's nemesis, The Crier, aka Francine McManahan. What were her real thoughts about the whole situation? She did act funny.

Recreating the scene in her head, Amelia remembered the tearful words The Crier had exchanged with her posse during Darcy Miller's bridal shower.

While the kids had retreated to their rooms to tackle homework, Amelia pulled out the telephone book. It was old-fashioned, but she thought she'd see if Francine McManahan was listed.

She couldn't be sure, but there was an F. McManahan listed in the gentrified neighborhood called Buck Town.

# Chapter Eleven

"I don't know, Lila. Something about that girl's behavior screamed guilty." Amelia told Lila her hunch about Francine. "I'm not saying I'm one hundred percent right, but I think that maybe in a fit of rage, maybe under the influence of alcohol, maybe when her normal inhibitions were disabled, she let loose on the girl in a way she can't take back."

"Really?" Lila asked, licking some frosting from her fingers before she went to the sink to wash them.

"I'm just guessing. But it is so strange that in the middle of a crowded party with not only guests walking around but also staff and extras like us, that nobody saw anything."

"Yeah, I know. That is more than a person can be expected to swallow."

"That means someone at that party had to see something, and they aren't telling." Amelia wiped the tip of her nose with the top of her hand, getting flour on it as usual. "Did I tell you I've got a new recipe I'm going to try?"

"No." Lila smiled. "What is it?"

"Orange brandy cupcakes." Amelia proudly lifted her chin.

"That sounds amazing," Lila encouraged.

"Yes, I thought I'd add a little grown-up flavor to them. I got the idea at the shower, believe it or not. Being at the bar and seeing all those intoxicated ladies having such a good time until...well, you know."

"The grisly homicide. Yeah. That does have a way of putting a damper on things. Did John have anything to say about it?"

"The cupcakes or the murder?"

Lila had learned quickly over the past several weeks that Amelia and John had some major differences in their perception of things that made the road to disagreements that much easier. She laughed at Amelia's sarcasm.

"The murder."

"You know, nothing different than usual. It's weird. When we were still married, he had no problem leaving the kids and me for days at a time without a security system. Of course we never had a gun in the house. The kids walked to and from the bus stop alone. Now, all of a sudden, he's so concerned about their safety he insists that Meg can't work with me. He makes sarcastic comments about it all the time." Amelia flopped down on the chair next to the counter where they prepared the raw cupcakes.

"Normally, if he were still your husband, I'd say do whatever you have to to make peace in the house. Sometimes that requires compromise and losing out a little." Lila smiled her gap-toothed grin at Amelia. "But the SOB left. He has no idea anymore who Meg is because he's not seeing her grow a little more every day. He only sees a little snapshot of her on every other weekend."

"Did I tell you he told Adam he could have a birthday party at the Windham downtown?"

Lila's drawn-on brown eyebrows shot up into the middle of her forehead.

"Really?"

Amelia repeated the story of her discussion with Adam during the bridal shower and how the whole idea was put in the boy's head.

"I'm trying not to blame Jennifer, Lila. Really, I am. She isn't the one who cheated. John is. She just... saw an opportunity, I guess." Amelia looked down at the floor. "But I don't want her putting in her two cents when it comes to the kids. Is that wrong? Am I being selfish or jealous?"

"No. She's just a kid herself. She doesn't know what she doesn't know. She's talking from the perspective of being a teenager, not raising one."

"Yes, that's it." Amelia pointed her finger at Lila while nodding her head. "But what do I do? I'll have to break Adam's heart. Like the kids haven't suffered enough. It's just that, starting him off with a party like that, what happens when he turns eighteen, then twenty-one? What is he going to want then?"

"I'd stick to my guns if I were you, Amelia. The thing to do is come up with a better alternative that both John and you can get behind. Pretend he's still your husband when it comes to issues with the kids. That might help."

Amelia narrowed her eyes and looked at Lila lovingly.

"That's excellent advice, Lila. Gosh, I just don't know what I'd do without you. Where were you when I was getting served divorce papers?"

"Excuse me, ladies," came the deep, familiar voice from the back of the truck. It was Detective Walishovsky.

"Dan, hi. What are you doing here?" Amelia asked, waving him in. He had to stand with his head bent down slightly in order to fit in the low-ceilinged space. Amelia felt Lila's eyes on her and just knew she was smiling that sly smile she gave her whenever the detective came around.

"It's official business. I was wondering, Amelia, if I could talk to you alone for a moment."

"Sure." She looked at Lila, who nodded her head and stood up, busying herself with folding and stacking more paper boats for the cupcakes and replacing the napkins while Amelia stepped off the truck with Dan.

"What can I help you with, Dan?"

"Actually, I just wanted to stop by and see how things were going. I felt bad how things ended the other night and..."

"My gosh, Dan, do you really think I gave it a second thought?" Amelia placed her hand gently on his arm. "You've got a job I couldn't begin to understand and a relationship with the other officers I'm totally clueless about. I just hope you won't hold it against a local yokel like me."

She blinked, looking up at him. The bright-blue sky, a rare thing in Oregon, was making her squint.

Dan looked down at her, and just the right corner of his mouth curled up.

"You are something special, Amelia." He looked at his watch.

"Has anything more come up in the case? Any leads?" Amelia looked at him curiously. She was sure he had talked to Tabitha Miller and Rusty. She wondered if Rusty had told him what he had told her about Dana's relationship with her uncle.

"We've got dozens of leads. Seems Miss Lila was right. We've found plenty of people with a motive. But they either weren't at the party or they were and could have someone testify to seeing them at all times. We've interviewed almost everyone."

"Almost everyone?"

"Yeah, there are two bridesmaids. The first is Francine McManahan. She's dodging us. The other is Sondra Collins, a police officer. She will probably say she was with Darcy the entire time. Then there is Mrs. O'Toole, who is at least two days older than Methuselah. It's a real puzzle."

"I'll bet." Amelia kept her thoughts to herself about Francine. She wanted to check things out on her own. Plus, no matter what Dan said, he'd wait to interview Sondra until all other options were exhausted. She knew this because if it was someone close to her, she'd do the same thing. "Would you like a cupcake for the road, Dan? You're looking a little malnourished."

"You know I can't say no. What's the flavor of the day?"

"Lemon poppy seed with a hint of almond." Amelia ran into the truck and quickly emerged with one of the giant cupcakes.

"You keep this up, Amelia, and you're going to make me a very fat man." He patted his stomach again, and Amelia was sure there was nothing but muscle there.

"So, just run a few extra laps at the gym," she joked as Dan left.

"Okay, what's the story?" Lila handed some change back to their latest customer, smiling kindly. "Come back and see us again." She waved good-bye then turned to face Amelia.

"He said they've got no leads. They interviewed everyone but, get this, Mrs. O'Toole, one of the female police officers who was there, and, hold on to yourself...Francine McManahan."

"Really?"

"Yup. I know. John has the kids this weekend. I'm going to try to bump into that girl. See what she has to say."

"Don't you think you should leave that to the police? If she's dodging them, then maybe she has something to hide. Maybe she's dangerous. Especially if she did do the deed. Are you sure you want to get that close to a throat slasher?"

"Nothing really fazes you, does it, Lila?" Amelia teased. "You can actually call someone a throat slasher and it appears to be no different than if you were calling them an Italian or an Englishman. A throat slasher. Yeah, could be."

"When you get to be my age, it's best to be blunt." She laughed. "Seriously, are you sure you want to run into her?"

"It'll be daylight. Lots of people," Amelia reassured Lila.

"Sure, just like the bridal shower?"

Lila's words sent a shiver up Amelia's spine.

# Chapter Twelve

Buck Town had been a very rough neighborhood for many years. The buildings were old and run-down, if not abandoned altogether. Graffiti was on the sides of every wall of brick, and the most unsavory characters took up residence in the structures owned by slumlords or provided by the taxpayers as affordable housing.

But slowly a new element started to buy up the property. A couple of nice restaurants had popped up. A retail shop or vintage store had opened here and there. And the old brownstones were being bought cheap and rehabbed only to be rented out or sold at a profit. Soon the elements that made the neighborhood unsafe were seeing more police on the street. The new neighbors didn't tolerate people loitering on street corners where they lived and their children played.

With a train to take people from Buck Town to the other hot spots in various Gary neighborhoods, the flow of people and money came pumping into the new area in gushes, attracting many affluent young people. Including people like Francine McManahan, who lived in a flat on the busy corner of Milwaukee and North Avenues.

Amelia didn't know if the "F." McManahan was indeed Francine.

"How many F. McManahans can there possibly be in Gary, Oregon? Or in the entire state, for that matter?" Amelia mumbled, alone in her car as she sat outside the apartment building she'd found listed in the phone book. Taking the Pink Cupcake truck would have been a little suspicious, so out came the old sedan in all its blahness. It was a cloudy day, and the clouds looked like they were about to crack open any second. That would be bad since Amelia might not be able to recognize The Crier if she was wearing a hoodie or tucked deep underneath an umbrella.

Thankfully, after her adventure with Detective Dan Walishovsky, she felt as prepared as any private detective. She had a thermos full of hot green tea. She had baked herself a special breakfast cupcake that consisted of a hash-brown base stuffed with scrambled eggs, finely diced peppers, a pinch of salsa, and crumbled bacon.

After easing her car into the shade underneath a massive oak tree, Amelia pulled out a tiny pair of binoculars from underneath her seat. They had been Adam's when he was going through his "spy stage" at the age of nine, asking for anything he could use to gather information secretly. They might not have been as fancy as Dan's, but they did the job well enough for her to see across the street. Pushing the seat all the way back from the steering wheel, Amelia got comfortable and waited.

It wasn't long before the front door opened up and the familiar face of The Crier, Francine McManahan, emerged from the building. She was not alone.

A man was with her who looked as if there were a dozen other places he'd rather be, including the morgue and the dentist.

However, Francine was fresh faced, talking and pulling on the man's arm, as if nothing were the matter. They walked in the opposite direction of Amelia's car.

"Okay, nothing too odd about that," she mumbled. Looking at the building and then at the couple as they disappeared, Amelia had a crazy thought.

"I'm not a person who does that," she stated. "I don't break into homes. I certainly don't break into homes of possible killers. And for all I know, Francine McManahan is one. No. I won't go break into her house."

She sat quietly for a few minutes.

"I could peek in some windows. That I could totally do. I'll just say I was looking for someone, if anyone asks." She climbed out of the car, still mumbling to herself. "If any do-gooder thinks they are helping by calling the police, I'm just looking for a friend of mine. They live on Polk. Wait, wait, what? This is Milwaukee? Polk is two blocks down? Oh, I'm so embarrassed. So sorry. I must look like a real doofus."

Sure, she mused. That would work in a pinch. Sure.

Climbing out of the car, she kept her eyes focused in the direction Francine and the man had headed. They must have rounded a corner, because they were nowhere to be seen. Looking up at the brownstone, she climbed the steps and, just to be sure, tried the front doorknob. Locked.

"Of course it is." She looked again down the street. No one seemed to be paying her any attention. Joggers were busy keeping their paces. Dog walkers were busy scooping poop. Everyone else was caught up on their cell phone or blocking out the world with earphones. For a moment, it seemed to Amelia she was the only one doing anything adventurous. It made her feel brave.

Slowly easing down the steps, Amelia quickly rounded the front of the building and slipped into the gangway. The windows were up too high for Amelia to reach. That was the intent of the architect, to help prevent burglars or transients from breaking in.

Around the back of the house was another door. Amelia walked up to it and found it locked, too. So much for her super sleuthing. Without another thought, she walked innocently back down the gangway, looking up at the windows, gauging whether or not she could jump and get a peek inside. As she rounded the front of the house, still looking up, she plowed right into Francine and the man.

"Oh my gosh!" Amelia started. "I'm so sorry."

"What are you doing? This is private property!" the man barked.

"I'm s-sorry. I was l-looking for 1818 Polk," Amelia stuttered, her nervousness genuine.

"Cole!" Francine piped up defensively. "Polk is two blocks over. This is Milwaukee."

Was this the one and only Cole Hansen? The Cole Hansen that Dana Foster had hoodwinked? It had to be, Amelia thought, remembering the scene Francine had made at the party, calling out his name.

"Oh, gosh. I'm so sorry." Amelia sighed. "I'm looking for an apartment that had a room for rent. No wonder I didn't see any sign. I'm sorry." Then Amelia stopped and looked at Francine. "You know, you look really familiar to me. Have we met before?"

The young woman looked at Amelia and squinted.

"I don't think so."

"Wait, you were at the party at the Twisted Spoke. And you stopped at my food truck just the other day."

Francine's eyes widened, and then she nodded her head. Cole looked at his watch.

"That's right. I'm sorry, Miss...?"

"Harley. Amelia Harley. What is your name?"

"Francine McManahan. This is my boyfriend, Cole Hansen."

Amelia reached out her hand to shake. Francine grasped her hand firmly, but Cole had quite a limp grip and let go of Amelia's hand almost instantly.

"That was some party, wasn't it? I don't know about you, but the police are still calling me." Amelia rolled her eyes.

"I'm going upstairs," Cole spouted, leaving the women and stomping up the cement stairs but not before giving Amelia a suspicious glare.

"I haven't spoken to any police. I didn't do anything," Francine spat quickly, her face contorting into a weird, snooty kind of smile.

"Neither did I. They just keep asking if I've seen anything," Amelia gushed, as if this was the most nerve-racking experience of her life. Little did Francine know this was not Amelia's first murder. That thought frightened Amelia. "I didn't even know the woman. Did you?"

"Look, I've got to get going. I've got things to do." Francine quickly cooled to Amelia's questions.

"I certainly didn't mean to keep you," Amelia apologized sincerely. "Please, come by the truck again sometime."

Francine barely gave Amelia a nod before she turned and hurried up the front stoop. Once she was inside, Amelia looked up at the building to see Cole staring down at her. Amelia waved but got no movement in response. Bending down to appear to be tying her shoe, Amelia waited, feeling Cole's eyes on her back. Then, just as she thought would happen, an argument ensued. The muffled words could still be heard at street level.

"Why are you talking to anyone about Dana?"

"I wasn't talking about Dana. That lady was selling cupcakes at the restaurant. If I didn't talk, it would have looked funny."

"You don't even know her."

"She's not a cop, obviously. She doesn't even know what street she's on."

"You don't find that suspicious?"

"No, I don't."

"Then you are dumber than she is."

"Ouch," Amelia growled. "No need to get personal. Sheesh." She stood up and walked down a block, away from Francine's place. Crossing the street, she made a beeline for her car, climbed in, and drove home.

Her mind was racing. Was Francine the one responsible for the brutal death of Dana Foster? Did she have enough anger and resentment toward the girl to kill her? Or did she do it for love? That Cole Hansen seemed pretty shaken up to see her talking to anyone about the incident. So much so that he must have planted the idea in her head to avoid the police.

When Amelia got home, she began to bake. Her idea for orange brandy cupcakes had been buzzing around in her head for too long. Now she really needed to process what she had just experienced with Francine and Cole. The best way to do that was to start baking in the kitchen.

The first batch contained enough brandy to get the taster a DUI if they were pulled over by the police. The second batch was just a plain old almond-flavored cake with a pungent orange aftertaste. But the third was heavenly.

A layered flavor of almond cake, a slight warmness from the brandy, and the pleasant aroma of orange that barely registered on the tongue made Amelia clap her hands as she ate three of them.

"Just a warm glaze over the top. Nothing heavy," she mumbled as cake crumbs fell from her mouth. "I am so good at this."

Smiling, she wrote down her list of ingredients and their amounts and prepared a list for the grocery store so she could stock up the truck.

"Come Monday morning, my customers will feel like they just slipped into a cozy log cabin with a warm fire burning, a glass of liqueur in a snifter, and the icy cold far away outside the windows, and all of this will be in their mouth." She laughed at herself.

She still hadn't decided what to do with her information on Francine and Cole. Truthfully, she didn't really have any information. She just had a hunch.

"I could call Dan." Her voice was loud in the empty house. Her kids would be home bright and early tomorrow, so if she was going to take any action, she'd better do it tonight.

Realizing it was just a little after noon, Amelia decided to keep the information to herself for the time being. Dana Foster would still be dead and Francine and Cole would still be suspicious for another twenty-four hours—or until she decided what to do next.

# Chapter Thirteen

"The website looks great!" Amelia gushed as Adam spoke with her on the phone. He had gone with his father to his law office. There, he went into the marketing department and was allowed to play around on some of the fancier computers used for design and promotional materials for the firm.

"I downloaded the pictures from the camera and was able to manipulate the images so you'd catch the details of the cupcakes in every frame. Plus, do you see how the cupcakes are more vivid while the images around them are just subtly blurred and darker? I did that, too."

"Honey, I can't get over this." Amelia was blown away. "Where did you learn how to do this stuff?"

"I picked it up on the streets," Adam teased.

"Now, does your computer do this or...?"

"No, Mom. I could go all tech geek on you, but I won't. Let's just say these are special designing computer programs that require a lot of space. My computers can't handle programs like this."

"Oh, okay. Yeah, don't go all tech geek on me." She studied the pictures and smiled. "You really caught some great shots at the party, too. You've got a natural eye to see things in a really artistic way. It's just beautiful, Adam, just..."

There it was.

Amelia squinted.

"Hey, Mom? Meg wants to know if Katherine can come over when we get back," Adam said while shushing his sister in the background.

"Yeah, sure. Hey, Adam. You said you darkened the backgrounds. Can you lighten something for me if I needed?"

"Sure, but you might lose the image in the foreground."

"That's okay." She told Adam what frame she was looking at and the particular part of the picture she wanted cleaned up. She was sure she knew what she was looking at but didn't dare just assume. "It doesn't have to be perfect. Just the best you can do, sweetie."

"Okay, Mom. I'll have it for you when I get home tomorrow."

Amelia quickly squeezed in a couple of "I love yous" to Adam and Meg, who was listening, before she hung up with them.

Scrolling through her updated website, she was thrilled at how professional it looked. Would anyone believe she had a sixteen-year-old as her designer?

Adam was very talented, but it was just sheer luck that he had snapped off a picture at the Twisted Spoke that could cause the whole case to crack wide open.

"See there?" Amelia was showing Lila the picture Adam had taken at the bridal shower that she requested he develop into a clearer image. He had made it crystal clear.

"That's the girl who threw the drink on Dana, for sure. But who is that guy?"

"That is Cole Hansen."

"What was he doing there?"

"We know he wasn't invited. It looks to me like he came in from the kitchen and not the main entrance, certainly not the open garage doors where the party was."

"So he snuck in and out without anyone knowing?" Lila shook her head.

"Well, I think Francine knew. I think she knew and maybe even put him up to it. There was something about the way they acted when I ran into them."

"Amelia, I'm going to be honest with you." Lila's face became long and concerned. "I don't think you should do any more without talking to Detective Walishovsky."

"I still could be wrong, you know." Amelia studied the picture. "Then I will have wasted his time, and he'll think I'm just some busybody jumping at every lead just to feel like I'm part of something big."

"I've never heard cops say they were upset to get leads, even if they turned out to be nothing." Lila wiped off the counter as she and Amelia got ready to open the truck. "I just don't want anything to happen to you. Not just because I could be out of a job but because you are my friend."

"Lila, you are so wonderful." Amelia hugged the older woman tightly. "I'm certainly not going to go throw myself into the lion's den. I've got kids to worry about and an ex-husband to show up. Plus, I like seeing you every day, too."

Lila laughed.

"Good. So long as your priorities are in line."

The women laughed and talked about how Cole Hansen could have gotten into the restaurant unnoticed. They talked about how Adam's work on the website captured the picture. Most importantly, they marveled over the new orange-and-brandy cupcakes they were making. As it turned out, the batches made in the truck were even better than the ones Amelia created alone in her kitchen.

"It's got to be the exhaust fumes that give it that extra something," Lila teased as she tasted another crumbled bit of sample.

"Something," Amelia concurred, but as she served her growing line of patrons, she couldn't help thinking of heading back to Buck Town and seeing what Cole and Francine were up to.

"I don't believe this." Lila shook her head. "We are out of everything. No more cupcakes and no more flour. That was a twenty-five-pound bag that we went through in less than a week."

"Let's call it a day." Amelia smiled as she hung the Closed sign on the open window and began cleaning up. Lila sat at the tiny counter and added the receipts for the day.

"How do we look?" Amelia finally asked after over twenty minutes of tallying.

"You're in the black again," Lila stated. "This is getting to be a habit with you."

"Let's hope."

As usual, Amelia waved good-bye to Lila, who walked home from Food Truck Alley every day to her high-rise apartment in the financial district just a couple of blocks away. With two solid hours before the kids came home, Amelia decided to head over to Buck Town and the mysterious apartment of Francine and Cole.

The chance of Francine being home was slim. She worked during the day, as she had said when she and her group of gals came to the truck.

Cole might have a different schedule. Either way, Amelia was determined to get inside that building and see what she could see.

"Francine isn't home," came the robotic-sounding voice through the intercom at the building on Milwaukee Avenue in Buck Town.

"That's really okay, Cole, because I'd like to talk to you," Amelia said, pressing the button so she could reply to him.

"Are you a cop?"

"No, and I'd like to avoid getting the police involved if they don't need to be." She tried to sound as kind as possible but was afraid she was sounding more like a blackmailer. Before she could say anything else, the connection went dead.

"So, I guess I will let Dan know about all this." Amelia found she spoke out loud to herself a lot and wondered if she always had or if it was a recent development. Before she got to the sidewalk, the door to the apartment building opened behind her.

# Chapter Fourteen

A very sour-looking Cole Hansen stood there in his bare feet, wearing a pair of jeans and a T-shirt.

"I've got five minutes before I have to check on the algorithms," he snapped.

"Algorithms? So you are a trader?" Amelia asked as she slowly climbed back up to the landing at the top of the stoop. Cole nodded, obviously annoyed.

"Well, I'll get right to the point." Amelia smiled sweetly. "What were you doing at the bridal shower where Dana was murdered?"

"I wasn't," he snapped again, looking at his watch.

"I don't think you want to play that game with me, Cole." She pulled out her phone and showed him himself in the background of one of Adam's pictures, clear as day.

All the color drained from Cole's face, and as Amelia looked down, she realized even his feet had gone ghostly white.

"Look, I didn't touch her. I just went to talk to her."

"During a bridal shower that your girlfriend was at?"

He ran his hand through his short blond hair and let out a grunt like a child told they couldn't watch any more television.

"Francine isn't my girlfriend anymore. She told me she was okay with being just friends."

"Then why did she say you were her boyfriend?"

Cole shrugged. "Out of habit, I guess. When she said she was going to that bridal shower, I knew Dana was going to be working that day."

"How did you know?"

"She told me." He sighed. "We had been together about a week before she was killed.

She said she made sure she was going to be on the schedule."

"Why did she want to work the bridal shower?"

"She didn't. She wanted to torture Francine." Cole was staring off behind Amelia, not looking at her eyes but past her as he spoke. Nervously, he worried a hangnail on his right thumb. "See, Francine and I had moved in together. It was too fast, and I wasn't ready to settle down. Then, when Dana stepped into the picture, I knew Francine wasn't right for me, but she said she was okay with being friends and that we could save some money by living together. No strings."

"So what did you show up there for?"

"To beg Dana not to bother Francine. I promised her she had my body and soul and that as soon as I got a few bucks saved up, I'd be back in my own place. She just needed to be patient."

"What did Dana say to that?"

"She said no. She said I wasn't going to stop her from having a good time. If I ever wanted to see her again, I'd just go home."

"So what did you do?"

"I came home." Cole's eyes became red, as if suddenly he was exhausted. "When Francine came home, she told me what had happened, and I died inside."

Amelia watched Cole calmly. She looked at his hands, his jaws, the way he moved, and came to the conclusion he was hiding something. She had seen on the true-crime television station that when a person lied, sometimes they fidgeted in addition to breaking out in a sweat or shifting their eyes all over the place. Cole showed all of the signs.

He bounced from foot to foot. He continued to pick at his thumb. His eyes bugged and squinted and searched all around, up and down the street, and as if that weren't enough, his upper lip began to glisten with sweat.

"So why haven't you gone to the police? This could be helpful."

He looked at Amelia, and his cheeks flushed with embarrassment.

"Francine will be upset."

Amelia didn't speak. She was mesmerized by his performance.

"I know what you're thinking. This guy is totally whipped." He whimpered. "Maybe, but if you heard the things Francine said she wanted to do to Dana, what she'd do to her herself, you'd think twice about talking to anyone, too."

"You're talking to *me*."

Cole chuckled.

"Yeah, and who are you? Nobody." He scoffed. "But if you're not a cop, I'd stay away from Francine. She might not look like much, but trust me, I know. You don't want to make her mad. She turns into a different person."

Amelia stood there as Cole quietly shut his front door. Taking a deep breath, she looked at her phone. It was time to head back home. The kids would be off school soon, and she'd planned hotdogs and salad for supper.

But as she drove, she couldn't shake the feeling that Cole was confused.

The drunken loudmouth at the bridal shower didn't strike her as a ruthless abuser, maybe even a killer, who instilled fear in anyone who crossed her.

For the entire drive back to her house, Amelia tried to make sense of everything Cole had said. If he wasn't her boyfriend, why did Francine introduce him as her boyfriend? Was she the split personality of a crybaby during the day and a homicidal girlfriend at night? What was Cole covering up?

"I'll never find out now," she sneered. She drove home on autopilot. Amelia took each turn and stop sign without even seeing them. Her mind spun Cole's words around and around, trying to see them from the correct angle, but everything seemed to have a blind spot.

Finally, when she did arrive home, she saw both Meg and Adam just getting off the bus. It was still very early in the day, and Amelia was thankful for the extra time she could spend with her kids. Perhaps giving her mind a break from the murder would help her see things more clearly later. She climbed out of the truck and waved to her kids.

"Hi, Mom!" Meg yelled as she ran up the sidewalk with Katherine following close behind. Adam sauntered coolly behind them, his skateboard under his arm as usual.

"Hello, girls. Did you have a good day at school?"

"Yes," they replied in unison and set off a chain of giggles. "How come you're home so early, Mom?"

"I had a good day at work. Sold out of everything." She stroked her daughter's long hair. Looking up at her son, she smiled. "How was your day, honey?"

"Good, Mom. What's for supper?"

"I thought hotdogs tonight. Salad. Maybe a movie while we eat?"

"Can we pick, please? Please, can we pick?" Meg pleaded, her hands folded in front of her as she batted her eyelashes at her mother.

"Adam, didn't Meg pick last time?"

"It's okay. I have a ton of homework." He looked at Meg and stuck his tongue out at her.

"Fine, spaz," she teased back. "He's just going to get on his computer and talk to Amy Leonard." Meg woo-hooed while flipping her hair back behind her. Adam shook his head and quickly went into the house. Amelia saw he had red cheeks but a smile on his face.

Amy Leonard came by almost immediately after Amelia and the kids had moved in to the small house as the divorce was wrapping up. She was a sweet girl with a skateboard and, as of recently, a streak of purple in her dark-brown hair.

"Leave your brother alone." Amelia tapped Meg on the head with her hand.

They made their way inside the house, and a feast of hotdogs with crisp green salad, crunchy potato chips, and iced tea was served while they finally agreed on a movie.

After shooting down Katherine's suggestions of *Dawn of the Dead*, *Carnival of Souls* or *The Incredible Melting Man*, which she insisted was a classic, they decided on Alfred Hitchcock's true classic, *Psycho*.

While watching with the girls, Amelia stared at the picture of Cole that Adam had sent to her. What else was there? He said he didn't do anything.

"Wait a minute!" she blurted out loud, making Meg and Katherine jump.

"What is it, Mrs. Harley?" Katherine asked nervously.

"Oh, nothing. I'm sorry. I was just remembering something from work that I thought I lost. I remember now. Never mind me."

"Jeez, Mom. Give us a heart attack."

Amelia nodded and shrugged her shoulders. Then she looked at the photo again. There it was. Peeking out of the corner was the top of someone's head. It was just a little old lady sitting in the back of the restaurant right next to the bathrooms. Mrs. O'Toole.

Dan had said he hadn't spoken to her yet because she was so old. Amelia remembered she had worn her raincoat inside the restaurant like a dress, then took it off after the temperature dropped and the rain started. Poor thing.

"You girls behave. I'm going to make a phone call, and I'll be right back."

"Okay, Mom," Meg said as she and Katherine scooted next to each other and, in whispers, wondered what was going to happen next as Janet Leigh got ready to take a shower.

Going upstairs into her room, Amelia pressed Dan's number that she had programmed into her phone, just in case there was an emergency.

"You've reached the voicemail of Detective Daniel Walishovsky. Please leave your name and number at the beep, and I'll call you back."

Amelia cursed the voicemail before the phone started recording her message.

"Hi, Dan. Um, it's Amelia Harley. Hey, I was just wondering if you had a chance to talk to Mrs. O'Toole about the Dana Foster case. The only reason I'm asking is because my son took a picture of the restaurant for my website, and it turns out she was sitting inside right next to the—"

Amelia frowned when she got cut off by the sound of the beep. She looked at the phone and debated calling back to leave the rest of her message but decided against it. He'd call back when he got a minute and ask what she was rambling on about.

In the meantime, Amelia wondered what she should do. A friendly visit to Mrs. O'Toole's might be in order. She knew the old lady from around town. Everyone did. You didn't have the kind of money she had and remain anonymous.

"A friendly visit. A wellness check. Heck, a bridal shower that could be featured on America's Most Wanted. I wish someone would have done a wellness check on me," Amelia joked.

Looking at her schedule, she thought that she might be able to swing by the old lady's house tomorrow afternoon and still make it home in time to get the kids dinner around five o'clock. She'd let them know she was going to be late taking care of some last-minute business. It wasn't a lie, but enough information was left out that they wouldn't worry or tell their father.

# Chapter Fifteen

"My gosh!" Lila said in a breathy voice. "You barely see her there."

"I know. She's like a chameleon blending in to the wood paneling. It's like *Where's Waldo?*" Amelia chuckled.

"I'll bet that Cole didn't even notice her, either. I'll bet he and Francine went ahead and slaughtered that girl, thinking no one was the wiser, and this old bird sat there listening to the whole thing, thinking it was just another symptom of her dementia."

"Lila"—Amelia bumped Lila with her hip, putting her hand over her own mouth to cover the laughter—"that isn't nice. And we don't know if she has dementia."

"I'm not trying to be mean," she reassured Amelia, bumping her back. "I'm just saying that she had to have heard something but might not believe she heard what she did."

Amelia clicked her tongue and shook her head.

"I hate to say it, but you might be right. I'm going to go talk to her."

"Are you going to wait for Detective Walishovsky to call you back? Maybe he already spoke with her."

"Well, if he did, then I'll just say *sorry to bother you* and run away out the door, waving my arms in the air like bees are swarming me." Amelia made herself and Lila laugh.

"I can just picture that," Lila whooped. "I'd pay money to see it live."

Both women laughed loud and hard as they opened the truck for business.

It was a rainy day, but the devoted customers of the Pink Cupcake cupcakes made their way through the elements, underneath their umbrellas and raincoats. Thankfully it was another sold-out event. Amelia had plenty of time to pay Mrs. O'Toole a visit and still get back in time to feed the kids.

"Look, just do me one favor," Lila said after packing up all the receipts in the bank bag and handing the money to Amelia. "When you get home, call me. Just so I know you are okay."

"Sure, Lila. But what could happen? Mrs. O'Toole is ancient. I'm probably going to go there and get stuck listening to her tell me how she acquired each one of her thirty cats."

"No! Is she a cat hoarder, too?"

"No. I'm making that up." Amelia hung her head. "I'm as bad as you are."

"Will you call me when you are done?"

"Absolutely. I plan on handing Dan some information he can use. I owe him."

"For what?"

"It's a long story, but let's just say he was right and I was wrong."

\* \* \*

Mrs. Belinda O'Toole had lived at 5726 North Winthrop Avenue in Sarkis Estates before the upscale neighborhood was even considered upscale. She and her husband had purchased a nice piece of property and had a New England Colonial–style home built on it. The place was three stories high and perfectly white with a jet-black roof that appeared to have been recently reshingled.

Amelia had stopped at home to drop off the truck. She didn't think it would be wise to drive her business to the woman's house. Not that the old sedan didn't stick out like a sore thumb in the fancy neighborhood, but it was certainly not the hot-pink beacon the Pink Cupcake was.

While in the car, Amelia went over what she was going to say, but none of it sounded right. It sounded like the ramblings of a crazy woman.

"Hi, Mrs. O'Toole. Do you remember going to the bridal shower the other day where there was a murder?"

"Mrs. O'Toole, I'm Amelia Harley. I was wondering if you remembered being at the Twisted Spoke when that little murder thing took place."

"Mrs. O'Toole, do you remember seeing this man go into the ladies' room just before Dana Foster was killed?"

That was it. It was blunt, but sometimes when dealing with the elderly, that was a person's best bet. Parking her car, she took a couple of deep breaths and headed up the porch steps to the front door. The curtains and blinds were pulled shut.

Looking up, Amelia saw they were shut on the second floor as well.

*Nothing strange about that,* she mused. *An old woman living alone with a rumor of gold bars buried in her walls probably enjoys the solitude.*

The door was hard wood with beautifully etched and beveled glass. She imagined the prisms on the floor had to look beautiful when the morning sun came through.

Pressing the button on the left side of the doorframe, she heard the doorbell ring on the inside. She hoped she wasn't disturbing anything.

It wasn't but a few seconds before Mrs. O'Toole was at the door, pressing her face into the glass and squinting. She looked like a pink and wrinkled gargoyle through the cut glass.

"Who is it?" she yelled through the door.

"Mrs. O'Toole, I'm Amelia Harley. Can I talk to you for just a minute?"

Mrs. O'Toole was shaking her head and mumbling something as she pulled away from the door. Amelia could hear the old woman complaining as well as the sound of several locks and chains sliding out of place.

When she pulled the door open, Mrs. O'Toole looked much more pleasant.

She was barely five feet tall. Her body was plump but not terribly overweight, and she reminded Amelia of her neighbor's pug dogs when they watched their master eat, with her shoulders slightly rounded over, her brown eyes peering from beneath wrinkle upon wrinkle. Amelia didn't think she dieted, especially after having watched her eat the cupcakes she made at the shower. She was probably just one of those lucky women who ate but never went too far over the edge.

"Yes, what is this about?" the woman asked, completely coherent and lucid.

"I'm sorry to bother you, Mrs. O'Toole. My name is…"

"Amelia Harley. Heard you the first time," she curtly replied. "Don't stand outside on the porch like a vacuum salesman. Come on in." She never cracked a smile.

Amelia realized she had labeled this woman totally wrong. Instead of the frail, rambling old lady she had expected, Mrs.

O'Toole was quite together. In fact, Amelia felt a little intimidated by her.

"Yes, well, I was wondering if I could ask you something about the bridal shower at the Twisted Spoke."

"Yes, what about it?"

She didn't seem fazed or even concerned about recalling that day's events.

"Well, you see, my son took a photo, and it just happened to catch a man going into the ladies' room right after Dana had gone in there. Then, Dana never came out. The top of your head was in that picture. I was just wondering if you remember seeing that man or hearing anything strange."

It was in a blink that Mrs. O'Toole's demeanor changed. The old lady smiled, but it looked more like a grimace.

# Chapter Sixteen

"Oh, that was a bad day, wasn't it?" Mrs. O'Toole tsk-tsked. Amelia watched as she waved her into the parlor. Before her eyes, Amelia thought the woman had grown about four inches and become more solid in frame. Not plump as she had thought before but sturdy. "Please, have a seat." She motioned to a beautifully upholstered sofa that had vibrant orange and pink flowers swimming through a sea of lush green leaves.

Amelia looked around the room and could only take a wild guess as to what everything had cost. If there were gold bricks in the walls, they were worth at least as much as what looked like a genuine Picasso and dozens of Capodimonte figurines.

The wallpaper was a silk floral design that complemented the bold print of the sofa and love seat that Mrs. O'Toole sat down on across from Amelia.

"This is a lovely room." Amelia smiled a nervous smile at her hostess, who appeared to be studying her.

"Thank you. Now, you said your son took a picture of me?" Mrs. O'Toole snooped. "Does he often take pictures of people he doesn't know?"

Her tone made Amelia jerk back just slightly.

"It was completely by accident."

Her nails were a bright orange color, but Amelia couldn't help noticing there were three severe gashes on her right index finger.

"My gosh," Amelia gasped. "What happened to your hand?"

"You are very interested in my well-being, Miss Harley, for someone who never met me before." Mrs. O'Toole's jaws pulsed like she might have been chewing gum, but

Amelia didn't think people with dentures usually chewed gum.

"I'm sorry. They just look like very deep cuts and..."

"You said your son had photos of me." Amelia was sure Mrs. O'Toole sneered as she said the word "son."

"He didn't take pictures of you. You were accidentally caught in the frame. Just the top of your head, really, in the corner of one of the pictures he took at the Twisted Spoke."

Mrs. O'Toole sat straight and still, all the while staring at Amelia.

"Well, what I wanted to ask you was, did you see this man go into the ladies' room there?" Amelia retrieved the picture from her purse. "I mean, it's fine if you didn't. No one else noticed him, either, but I thought since you were so close that maybe you caught a glimpse of him."

Still Mrs. O'Toole stared, and for a few seconds, Amelia thought she was having some kind of seizure or episode.

"You know the Fosters live next door to me." Mrs. O'Toole finally spoke, letting Amelia hang there with the picture in her hand.

Amelia's eyes widened.

"Why, no. I had no idea. Well, that is weird, isn't it?"

Mrs. O'Toole smirked, imitating Amelia's surprised reaction.

"That little girl of theirs was rotten from the word go."

"I hate to say that I've heard a lot of that over the past few days." Amelia tried to sound lighthearted, but it wasn't working at all. Her voice was betraying her by cracking and wavering, and her mouth had gone completely dry.

"Mrs. Harley, do you have money?"

"What?"

"What am I saying? I see your car out there. Obviously not. You work at that food truck stand."

"I own it," Amelia corrected. Insulting her finances was one thing, but insulting her business...that was another.

"Your cupcakes are okay."

"I noticed you ate two of them." Amelia tried to smile her nerves away, but Mrs. O'Toole made sure they stayed taut and trembling.

"You see, Mrs. Harley, when you have money like I do, there is always someone sniffing around who feels they are entitled to some of it."

"I can assure you, Mrs. O'Toole, I don't want your money. In fact, I think I've wasted enough of your time." Amelia stood from the sofa, stuffing the picture back into her purse then wringing her hands.

"Sit down, Mrs. Harley, or I'll shoot you where you stand."

"Shoot me?" Amelia breathed the words as she watched Mrs. O'Toole pull a small revolver out from behind one of the cushions on the love seat she was sitting on.

"Yes, shoot you! Are you deaf as well as dumb?" Mrs. O'Toole instantly changed in front of Amelia. She became a dangerous beast, completely unpredictable and terrifying.

Amelia clutched her purse.

"It's funny how you come here with a picture in your hand you want me to look at. Just like that girl did."

"What girl?" Amelia shook her head. "Mrs. O'Toole, I can assure you that I have no idea what you're talking about, but if you put down the gun, we can get you some help. We could go out on the porch and call whoever you like and..."

"You're just like her. She thought I was just some senile old coot, too." Mrs. O'Toole stood up, still pointing the gun at Amelia. She had become a monolith casting Amelia in a very dark shadow. "Suffering from dementia." She grinned wildly, pulling her lips back so her teeth and gums were glistening in the afternoon light.

"Mrs. O'Toole, I'm not here to hurt you."

"Of course you're not," she hissed. "That was what Dana said to me, too, the day she sauntered into my home, wearing a skirt so short she might as well not have worn anything, and showed me the pictures she had taken!"

"What pictures, Mrs. O'Toole?"

"Why, the pictures of my husband, of course."

Swallowing hard, Amelia looked around, half expecting Mr. O'Toole to come skulking around a corner with some look of madness on his face, too.

"Don't worry. He's not here."

Maybe he wasn't crazy. Maybe if she could keep Mrs. O'Toole talking, Mr. O'Toole would come home from whatever game of golf or cocktail hour he was at and help get her out of this mess. But Mrs. O'Toole was reading her mind.

"Well, he's here in the basement, but he won't be coming up," Mrs. O'Toole said. "He died some time ago."

Amelia's head spun and her stomach lurched as her mind tried to make sense of the nonsense she was hearing.

"That was what that horrible beast wanted to show me." Mrs. O'Toole clenched her teeth. "Dana Foster had taken pictures through my basement window."

Mrs. O'Toole's hand began to tremble with rage as she told Amelia about that horrible day.

Dana Foster had come to the door with pictures of Mr. O'Toole's dead body just propped up in a corner of the basement. She told Mrs. O'Toole she was planning on robbing her, breaking in through one of the basement windows to steal whatever she could, maybe find a gold bar or two buried in the walls, but she thought why steal when she could just have Mrs. O'Toole give her money when she wanted.

"She said she'd go to the police if I didn't pay her one hundred thousand dollars...for starters."

Amelia found herself almost laughing as she pondered who was worse, Mrs. O'Toole for leaving her dead husband in the basement or Dana for knowing he was there and asking for money not to tell anyone.

"I'm sure you're wondering why my husband is down there," Mrs. O'Toole snapped.

Amelia suddenly felt like a thousand spiders were crawling up her legs as she thought of Mr. O'Toole's decaying body lying somewhere beneath her in the darkness of the basement. She shivered, and it made Mrs. O'Toole giggle with insane glee.

"He hadn't done a thing. I was just tired of him," she snarled. "Every day he did the same things, wore the same clothes, talked about the same topics, and was always the expert. Do you know this room had been all white for over thirty-five years because he refused to allow me to change it? All white for all those years made me feel like I was in an institution. See what some color can do? You, yourself, just complimented me on it."

That must have scored some kind of brownie point because Mrs. O'Toole seemed to puff with pride.

"Mr. O'Toole was much larger than me. However, he wasn't larger than a monkey wrench to his head. It was rather anticlimactic, to tell the truth. He just crumpled to the ground. End of story." She let out a sigh. "So, I thought if it were good enough for my husband of over forty years, it was better than that little hussy deserved."

Amelia's mouth had gone slack. She sat stone still, feeling a cold sweat develop down her spine and under her arms, but she didn't dare tremble.

"It's rather funny," Mrs. O'Toole said, more to herself than Amelia. "She was so absorbed in her phone that she didn't even see me come up behind her. The woman who had been paying her over five thousand dollars a week for the past several months and she doesn't even look up."

"You slit her throat and stabbed her, too," Amelia muttered, surprised she could even find her own voice. "That's how you cut your fingers."

"I'll admit I got a bit carried away. I didn't expect the opportunity to arise the way it did." She looked at Amelia like she was a piece of meat. "Just like this one."

"Mrs. O'Toole, please." Amelia put her hands out defensively. "I have children. They need me."

"You should have just run out the door, then, because now that you know everything, I can't let you live. They'll get over it." Mrs. O'Toole cocked the pistol. "It's a shame I have to use a gun. We've shared so much, it feels, I don't know, cold."

"People know I'm here, Mrs. O'Toole! They'll come looking for me! They'll see in the basement even if they don't figure out what you did to Dana!"

"What? I'll tell them you were here." Mrs. O'Toole became a fragile, sweet old lady in front of Amelia's eyes. "Yes, Amelia Harley. She stopped by. Pretty woman, about forty, with a short haircut. Yes, she came by, and we chatted about some man in a picture she was asking me about. Then she left. Why, has something happened to her?"

Like Dr. Jekyll and Mr. Hyde, she morphed into the heartless hag again.

"I'm sorry, Mrs. Harley. You should have tended your own yard."

Knock, knock, knock.

Amelia held her breath. Mrs. O'Toole froze, her lips drawing down at the corners into a fierce growl.

"Don't move." She mouthed the words.

Immediately Amelia lunged for the side table next to her, grabbed a Capodimonte figurine of a cherub-faced boy climbing up a tree, and whipped it against the wall. It shattered into a million pieces, echoing like thunder through the house as it crumbled onto the hardwood floor.

"Help!" Mrs. O'Toole cried. "Oh, help me!" She thrust the gun deep into her right pocket and, without a moment's hesitation, threw herself violently to the floor, causing the paintings on the wall to rattle.

Before Amelia could dash to the door, it came crashing in. She recognized the shoe.

Out of breath and alert, Dan burst into the home, his gun drawn.

"Police!" His voice was a choir of angels to Amelia, who froze and put her hands up. Mrs. O'Toole writhed on the floor.

"Stop her!" Mrs. O'Toole whimpered. "She's trying to hurt me."

Tears streamed down Mrs. O'Toole's face. She huddled close to the wall, crying like a dog that had been beaten.

"What in the world is going on?" Dan kept his gun drawn, unsure if he should keep it on Amelia or the old woman or if there was someone else in the house.

"Dan, don't let her go! She killed Dana and her own husband!"

"What?" Dan barked.

"She's got a gun!" Amelia cried just as Mrs. O'Toole was reaching inside her pocket.

"Don't move!" Dan yelled at Mrs. O'Toole.

"But I need my pills," she gasped.

"She doesn't have pills, Dan! She's got a gun!" Amelia charged in front of Dan just as Mrs. O'Toole withdrew her pistol and got one shot off.

# Chapter Seventeen

Amelia woke up in a beige room and heard a steady beeping in her left ear. Fluttering her eyes open wide, she was hit with a massive headache. When she tried to push herself up, her left arm stung like a swarm of fire ants were giving her a go.

"Ouch." She gritted her teeth.

"You're awake."

Clutching her heart with her right hand, Amelia let out a yelp of surprise.

"Dan. Geez, where am I?"

"You're in the hospital."

"What for?"

"Well, first, you got shot. Luckily it was just a graze on your left forearm. The doctor sewed you up in about three minutes."

"And second?" She rubbed her head and winced at the giant goose egg that was there. "Ouch!" She gritted her teeth again.

"You fell and hit your head against an oak side table. The doctor wanted to keep you here for observation."

"My gosh!" Amelia almost began to cry. "My kids! Lila! Oh, they are going to be freaking out! I have to get home!" She tried to get up, but somewhere a giant crane tilted the room and gave it a good spin, sending her back to the pillow.

"Hold on." Dan stood up, his phone in his hand while he looked down quickly, texting something to someone. "They know where you are and that you're all right."

"How? Who told them? How did you get to Mrs. O'Toole's?"

"Well, you have a very concerned friend who gave me a call and told me what you were doing."

"Lila." Amelia sighed. Her face twisted into an embarrassed grin.

"Yes." Dan's voice was a whole octave lower. Amelia felt a lecture coming on. "Do you have any idea how dangerous it was for you to go over there?"

"I know." Amelia touched her head delicately with her finger. "Normally killers are so friendly and accommodating. Mrs. O'Toole had terrible manners."

"I mean it." Dan sat down on the edge of the bed. "You've got a family to think about. Not to mention all the people who eat your cupcakes." He patted his stomach.

"Gosh. How am I going to get to work in time tomorrow?" She sighed again. "I did make a mess of things."

"Actually, Miss Bergman gave me a message to give to you. She said not to worry, she hired a temp to take up the slack while you're off tomorrow."

Amelia's mouth fell open.

"Who?"

Dan shrugged but was smiling.

"Oh, I don't care." Amelia pouted, folding her arms across her chest. Peeking up from beneath her lashes, she looked at Dan. "So, where is Mrs. O'Toole now?"

Dan admitted to Amelia that the old woman hadn't even been on the police department's radar until he looked up her address.

As Mrs. O'Toole had mentioned, she had been neighbors with the Fosters for a couple of decades. Still, she was old and frail, or so they thought.

Dana's parents had been traveling abroad and had just arrived home within the last couple of days. Dan made a trip to their house yesterday not only to offer his condolences but also to question them, to look in Dana's room, to try to get an idea of who might have done this to her.

"At first I was sure it had to do with some jilted fellow," Dan admitted. "But then I found her stash of pictures."

"Stash?"

Dana had pictures of herself with several young men, and not-so-young men, from around town that their significant others would not approve of. She also had pictures of spouses behaving badly. And then there were the pictures from Mr. O'Toole's basement.

"Dana's parents had tried to cut her off. They tried disciplining her, giving her a tight allowance, but she would always find a way to get money. The Fosters had assumed it was the old-fashioned way," Dan said, giving Amelia a raised-eyebrow look.

"The oldest profession?"

Slowly he nodded his head.

"Turned out not to be the case. She was blackmailing half the people on her own block."

"You mean she wasn't the floozy everyone thought she was?" Amelia stuttered.

"No, she was. Most definitely," Dan said, standing up from the bed. "She just made sure no one got something from her for nothing."

"Yikes."

"Mrs. O'Toole proved to be an even bigger player than Dana." Dan loosened his tie and unbuttoned the top button of his collar. "When you have the beauty of youth going up against plain old-fashioned experience, I put my money on experience every time."

Dana thought she had Mrs. O'Toole wrapped around her finger. The idea that Mrs. O'Toole was, in fact, a cold-blooded killer didn't seem to sink in to Dana's pretty head.

To her, knowing such a big secret about one of the richest people in town— one who had one foot in the grave and another on a banana peel—made Dana feel she was in charge. She just didn't think of the reality that if Mrs. O'Toole had killed the man she married, why would she care about killing some girl who was too big for her britches and who was hated by most everyone around town?

"Did you know it was Mrs. O'Toole?"

"We didn't at first, but thanks to that guy, Rusty, who kept the crime scene clean, we were able to find one perfect footprint left behind by the killer."

"What luck!" Amelia shook her head in awe.

"Well, a lot of times, that's what this business is." Dan walked over to the window and opened up the curtains. The sun was setting, and the colors looked pretty to Amelia, who winced again as she scooted up in the bed. "The footprint was in a style of shoe not worn by the majority of women who attended the party. You know, those flat, thick-soled athletic shoes. There was only one other person who might wear them, but we ruled her out immediately."

"Who was that?"

"You."

"Me?" Amelia laughed out loud then rubbed her aching head.

"Yeah." Dan gave Amelia a wink. "Then Darcy went through the guest list with me, letting me know who she thought could have been wearing a comfortable shoe like that. Mrs. O'Toole was the most likely."

Dan went on to say that after Amelia knocked herself out, they subdued Mrs. O'Toole and made a search of the house. Not only did they find the shoe with Dana's blood on it but they also found a monkey wrench that had dried blood on it.

"That would be her husband's." Amelia sighed.

"Not that we need the murder weapon. In the search for the shoes, we found his body in the basement."

"My gosh. What kind of a person does that?" Amelia's mind couldn't comprehend it. She decided she didn't even want to try. The thought that she could have ended up down in that desolate, sad basement, too, was too close. "How long had he been down there?"

"If I had to guess, it was about ten months, maybe a year."

"Dan, the smell. The bugs. All of that so she could put wallpaper up?"

"What?" Dan leaned against the ledge of the window, crossing his arms.

Amelia went on to tell him the story Mrs. O'Toole had shared with her about the white walls and the wrench.

"I hate to say this, but I don't know which one of them was worse, Dana Foster or Mrs. O'Toole."

"Well, Mrs. O'Toole will be facing her judgment soon enough. I see this as a slam dunk."

Amelia thought that Dana was also facing her judgment. It made her shiver.

Before either of them could speak again, the phone rang. Amelia went to reach for it, squinting her eyes as if that somehow could ease the pain.

"Hello?"

"Mom?" It was Adam's voice. He sounded like that little boy who had held her hand tightly in the parking lot. "Are you okay?" The worry in his voice was like a slap against Amelia's heart.

"Honey, I'm fine. I'm so sorry," she soothed. "Is your sister there? Tell her that I'm fine and I'll be home tomorrow."

She heard Adam repeat the words to his sister in the background.

"What happened? Did you really get shot?"

"It isn't like you think. It's more like a really bad scratch, that's all."

Again Adam reported the details to his sister.

"Mom, we called Dad. He said..."

"Don't tell me what he said, honey. I'll give him a call myself and let him know that I'm bulletproof." She chuckled a little for Adam's sake.

"Mom?" Meg must have wrestled the phone from her brother. "Lila is here. She said she was going to take us for pizza."

"Well, isn't she the sweetest thing?"

"And she said not to worry about the truck. She's got someone who can help, and you won't even miss a day. Just enjoy your hospital food and relax."

"Would you tell Lila I owe her, *again*."

Meg relayed the message, and there was something said that made her fourteen-year-old daughter laugh. It sounded like music.

"We were really worried about you, Mom. I think Adam and I are going to have to think of an appropriate punishment. Grounding may not be enough."

"Oh, great. Well, I'll take my lumps." She looked at Dan and smiled. "I'm grounded."

"Can you have visitors? I may have to stop by and check on you."

Amelia felt her cheeks turn red.

"Okay, Mom. We'll see you tomorrow. Get some rest."

"I love you both. Tell your brother."

"I will."

"Tell him now."

"Mom," Meg whined.

"Would you please?" Amelia laughed.

"Ugh, Adam, Mom says she loves you. Ick. There. Happy now?"

"Very. See you guys tomorrow."

Hanging up the phone, Amelia told Dan that Lila was with her kids. Her voice trembled a little as she told him a little more about them, their personalities, and how their hobbies suited them.

"Adam will be thrilled at what a big part his photo played in apprehending a murderer."

"Adam what?" John stepped into the hospital room, his face drawn and pale.

"John? What are you doing here?" Amelia straightened in the bed, barely aware of the pain.

"The kids called and told me you got shot." He panted as if he were upset the wound wasn't more serious.

"Detective Dan Walishovsky, this is my ex-husband, John." Dan stood straight and offered his hand to John, who shook it quickly, barely looking at Dan's face.

"Nice to meet you," John growled as he stared at Amelia. "So, what happened?"

Amelia looked apologetically at Dan, who nodded and gave her a discreet wink.

"I'll check on you later. Thanks again, Amelia. We couldn't have solved this without you." Jerking his chin up at John, Dan left the room.

"Now, before you get crazy, John, let me tell you that the kids were not in any danger and..."

"No, but their mother got shot."

"I didn't get shot, John, the bullet just grazed me. Thanks to the fact the old lady's sight was going." Amelia batted her eyelashes.

John sat down on the side of the bed, shaking his head and clicking his tongue. He took Amelia's hand in both of his. They didn't speak.

"John?"

"If something happened to you...who'd take the kids?"

"What?"

John looked at Amelia.

"Jennifer and I are planning a future and..."

"John, you don't need to explain to me. I'm fine. The kids will be fine." She rolled her eyes and pulled her hand away. "Now that you're here, we need to talk about Adam's birthday. What is this talk about a party at the Windham?"

Amelia and John spoke for over an hour until the nurse stopped in.

"Our guest needs a little rest," the nurse chirped.

# Chapter Eighteen

When Amelia got home from the hospital—thanks to Dan, who offered to drive—she entered the quiet, empty house and immediately put on a pot of coffee.

"Would you like a cup?"

"I've got time for one." Dan stretched.

"Hey, what's going on with your stakeout?"

"Well, interesting thing. The pictures we got of Mick O'Donell and his partner's wife? Turns out his partner knew all about it."

"Yuck! Really?" Amelia gasped. "And he didn't mind? That's A-okay with him?"

Dan nodded his head while rolling his eyes. He pulled out a chair at the kitchen table and took a seat.

"My gosh." Amelia grabbed two coffee cups, cringing as she reached up to get them out of the cabinet. Her arm throbbed in the place where the two pieces of skin were stitched together, but already she thought it felt better than it had the day before. Her head still ached when she touched it, but the goose egg was now maybe the size of a golf ball at most. "What is wrong with people?"

"Right?" Dan watched Amelia as she bustled around. It was like her battery had been recharged. "You really know your way around a kitchen."

"I know my way around *my* kitchen," she joked while pouring him a hot cup of coffee.

"Truthfully, I'm a little anxious. I have no idea who Lila has covering for me today." Amelia pouted. "I trust Lila, who knows how to make a few of the basics, but someone else running around in my truck? It makes me feel like I'm wearing clothes that are two sizes too tight, you know?"

"Well, I wouldn't worry about it." Dan took a sip from his cup.

"You were right all along, Dan."

"About what?"

"About knowing that it wasn't one of your officers who committed that murder. You were one hundred percent right, and I'm sorry for doubting you."

"No apology is necessary," Dan grumbled bashfully. "I'll tell you what. If you ever decided to give up the cupcake business, I think the Gary Police Department could use a gal like you."

"A *gal* like me?"

"You could come on a couple of ride-alongs with me. You're certainly better company than Gus."

"Does he know you talk about him this way?"

"Of course he does."

"Well, I don't think I would want to be your partner. You'd always be talking smack about me. 'Did you see Amelia? She got shot in the arm then knocked herself unconscious. Boy, what I have to deal with.'"

Dan laughed out loud. It was the first time Amelia had ever seen a genuine smile or heard a real laugh from the serious detective. It was contagious. She laughed, too.

After talking about Mr. O'Toole, Dana Foster, and the Twisted Spoke, Dan looked down at his watch and let out a deep breath.

"Well, I guess I better get going. The chief is going to expect me to punch in sometime today. What's that saying? Crime never takes a holiday?"

"Oh, okay," Amelia replied disappointedly. "Thanks again for bringing me home. I would have been in a bit of a jam if you hadn't. I appreciate it."

"My pleasure," Dan said, thrusting his hands into his pockets as he strolled to the front door.

"I never thanked you." He looked at the floor as his left hand found the doorknob.

"Thanked me? For what?"

"For saving my life. You pushed me out of the way of that bullet. Mrs. O'Toole was going to get one or both of us, but your quick thinking saved us both. So, thank you."

Dan pulled the door open but, before stepping outside, leaned down and kissed Amelia on the cheek. She stood in the doorway and watched him stroll to his car, wearing that plain brown suit like he usually did, his hard-soled shoes clacking against the pavement. Before he slipped his tall frame behind the wheel, he gave Amelia a wink and a wave.

She smiled broadly and waved back.

# Chapter Nineteen

It had been over four months since the shoot-out with Mrs. O'Toole. The newspapers had dubbed her the Gray Widow because she was an old lady who killed people.

Amelia tried, with Dan's help, to keep her own name out of the papers, but a few blurbs snuck in stating she was the one who had narrowly escaped the spider's web.

"It's such a gross comparison," Amelia said as she frosted the cupcakes for Adam's birthday party. Instead of silver and black like they had been for the ladies at the Twisted Spoke bridal shower, Amelia made them a neon green and gray. They looked like fireworks in your hand. "Gray Widow. Anything associated with spiders is gross."

"Well, thankfully it's all over." Lila comforted her friend as she scooted around her to empty a giant bag of potato chips into a neon-green bowl.

"Mom!" Meg yelled from the open back door. "Where are the cupcakes? The peasants are threatening to revolt!"

"I'm coming!" Amelia yelled back. "Just give me a few more minutes."

She looked at her watch and then the clock over the microwave.

"Where is he?"

"He'll be here," Lila soothed. "You talked to him, right?"

"Yes, I did. I'm just nervous. I can't wait to see Adam's face."

"You never told me what John said to you after the shooting." Lila looked at Amelia down her long, thin nose. "Did he have a lot to say?"

Amelia hadn't told Lila anything because she knew Lila's opinion of her ex-husband already. It was just a shade darker than Amelia's, but if she told her that John's primary concern was about himself, she'd hit the roof. Plus, holding on to that kind of information was hard. Amelia didn't want to risk Lila slipping and saying something in front of the kids.

It would break their hearts if they knew the only reason their dad came to visit her in the hospital was to make sure they wouldn't be his responsibility.

"You know, that same old stuff about being responsible. How it makes him look. Nothing even worth repeating."

"Well, I'm surprised he's here," Lila said, looking out the kitchen window.

"He wouldn't miss Adam's birthday. Not when he gets a chance to show off like this."

"Yeah, but it was a great compromise." Lila turned and helped herself to a handful of M&M's. "To have the birthday party at your house then take the money they would have wasted at the Windham and buy him all those new upgrades and gadgets he likes? That was brilliant."

"Sure was. My idea. All mine." Amelia stooped over the counter to add a green candy jewel to the center of each cupcake. "His room in the basement is going to look like NORAD."

"Well, you can stop looking at the clock," Lila mumbled. "I think he's here."

Amelia stood up, smoothed her short hair at the nape of her neck, and pulled the wrinkles out of her shirt. Looking at Lila, who gave her the okay sign, she smiled and peeked around the corner toward the front door.

"Hi!" she called. "I was worried you might not make it."

Dan grinned down at Amelia. He was carrying a brightly colored bag with tissue paper and bows hanging off the handle. It was the perfect contrast to his suit that was a light-gray pair of slacks and matching jacket.

"Just some last-minute paperwork." He handed the bag to Amelia. Looking up, he waved at Lila. "Good to see you, Miss Bergman."

"You too, Detective."

"Okay, well, Adam and all of his friends are out back roasting marshmallows around the fire pit. John is out there with them. I guess it's time he open his gifts."

"Hi, Detective! Mom, are you ready?"

"Gosh, yes, Meg." Amelia huffed awkwardly, lifting the platter of cupcakes. Dan took it from her with ease and followed her and Lila out into the backyard, where everyone began to sing *Happy Birthday*.

# Recipe 1: Peanut Butter and Jelly Cupcakes

*Makes 12*

## Ingredients:

- 1 ½ cups all-purpose flour
- 1 cup granulated sugar
- 2 large eggs
- 1 egg yolk
- 1 cup grape jelly
- ¾ cup milk
- 1 teaspoon baking powder
- ½ teaspoon salt
- 1 stick (4 ounces) unsalted butter, room temperature
- 2 teaspoons pure vanilla extract

## Peanut Butter Frosting:

- 2 cups icing sugar
- 1 1/2 teaspoons milk
- 1/2 cup smooth peanut butter
- 4 tablespoons unsalted butter, room temperature
- 4 ounces cream cheese, room temperature

Preheat oven to 350 degrees F. Line muffin tin with 12 cupcake liners. Sift flour, baking powder, and salt in one bowl. In another bowl, use a hand mixer on medium speed to cream butter and granulated sugar until light and fluffy. Beat in eggs, egg yolk, and vanilla extract. Reduce speed to low. Pour in milk. Continue to mix until smooth. Gradually add dry ingredients into the mix until blended.

Spoon batter evenly into prepared cups, about ¾ full. Bake for 20 minutes, or until tops of cupcakes spring back and are not too golden. Let cool for 15 minutes. Before adding filling or frosting, let cupcakes cool on rack completely.

Fill a squeeze bottle with jelly and close cap. Insert tip of bottle deep into the tops of the cupcakes. Squeeze about 1 tablespoon of jelly inside each cupcake.

Use the Peanut Butter Frosting to cover the top.

### Peanut Butter Frosting:

Beat peanut butter, butter, and cream cheese on medium speed until light and fluffy. Slowly add the icing sugar and mix until smooth. Add milk and continue to mix until the frosting becomes a good spreading consistency.

# Recipe 2: Apple Crisp Cupcakes

*Makes 12*

## Ingredients for Cupcake:
- 2 eggs
- 1 ½ cups all-purpose flour
- 1 cup sugar
- 1 apple, peeled, cored, and diced
- 1/2 cup butter, melted and cooled slightly
- 1/3 cup milk
- 1 ½ teaspoons baking powder
- 1/4 teaspoon salt
- 1/2 teaspoon vanilla

**Streusel:**

- 3/4 cup brown sugar
- 1 teaspoon cinnamon
- 3 tablespoons butter, room temperature
- Pinch of salt

**Frosting:**

- 3/4 cup butter, room temperature
- 3 cups icing sugar
- 1/4 cup apple butter
- 1 teaspoon cinnamon
- 1/2 teaspoon vanilla

Preheat oven to 350 degrees F. Line muffin tin with 12 cupcake liners. Mix flour, baking powder, and salt in a bowl. In another bowl, beat sugar, butter, eggs, and vanilla until smooth. Gradually beat in flour mixture and milk until smooth. Fold in apple.

**For streusel:** Hand whisk brown sugar and cinnamon in a small bowl. Add butter in small pieces until mixture is small, moist clumps. Use fingertips to mix butter in better if necessary.

**For Frosting:** Beat butter until smooth. Add in apple butter, cinnamon and vanilla, and finally sugar, until mixture is thick and smooth.

**Assembly:** Use half of the cupcake batter to fill 12 liners. Place some streusel on each one. Fill liners with remaining batter. Bake for 20-25 minutes or until toothpick comes out clean. Let cool in pan for 10 minutes, then let cool on cooling rack completely. Add frosting on top of cooled cupcakes.

A Deadly Bridal Shower

196

# About the Author

Harper Lin is the USA TODAY bestselling author of 5 cozy mystery series including *The Patisserie Mysteries* and *The Cape Bay Cafe Mysteries*.

When she's not reading or writing mysteries, she loves going to yoga classes, hiking, and hanging out with her family and friends.

**www.HarperLin.com**

.

Made in the USA
San Bernardino, CA
04 October 2016